Hidden

Book One

The Angels Evermore Series

By: Raven K. Asher

The Angels Evermore

Text copyright © 2014 Raven K. Asher

Updated and Edited November 2022

The Angels Evermore

Raven K. Asher

The Angels Evermore

"Hidden" Book 1

"Captured" Book 2

"Sacrifice" Book 3

The Angels Evermore

Table of Contents

Raven K. Asher

The Angels Evermore

Chapter One

Moving from town to town wasn't exactly my idea of a great summer vacation, but with how things were, Mom insisted that we had to move every summer.

It was an exhausting task, but we were pretty much used to it now.

We had been at this since I had turned twelve, and now I was only a week away from turning eighteen.

The towns had begun to blend into one another, and looking out my window now, watching the newest small town pass, I knew this town would be just like all the others.

We would live there, go to school, and then disappear.

Wash, rinse, and repeat.

Just once, I wished that we could stay in a single town instead of having to move over and over again, but it was far too dangerous for me to stay in a single place for too long.

My mom and sister, on the other hand, deserved more. They deserved not to have to move from town to town, always having to make new friends to lose them later on when we left again.

I felt like a burden to them, and just as soon as I was out of school, which would be this year, I would leave them so they could finally stay.

I would take my turn to run and run alone for once.

"Are you alright, Piper?" My mom, Helen, questions from the driver's side of the car, her long brunette hair waving in the wind from her window being rolled down.

Her blue eyes meet mine with concern, so I plaster on a fake smile.

"I'm fine, Mom." I lie easily.

Lying had become routine for me. What my mom and sister didn't know wouldn't hurt them. At least, that's what I forced myself to believe.

"Are you two excited to see our new place?" Mom asks with enthusiasm, to which my sister and I groan.

"Awe, come on, Piper, Hannah, you're going both love this house. We're even going to have neighbors." She adds with more excitement.

My head swings around from my watch out the window to meet her face, my eyes going wide with fear.

"Are you crazy, Mom? We can't have neighbors. It will be too hard to keep me a secret." I snip out.

She sighs loudly, her excitement diminishing within seconds.

"I just thought that...that maybe this once you could try a little harder to hide. I want to try for a more normal life here." She states gently.

Her words hit me like a ton of bricks, even though she wasn't trying to offend me.

I knew she was tired of moving, but there it was, in her own spoken words. It was clear that I had to get away from them this year. I had to allow them the freedom that I could never have.

"Well, I think that having neighbors for once will be awesome. Are there any cute guys?" Hannah squeals from the backseat abruptly.

Glancing back, I watch her flip her hair over her shoulders as she sits up straighter to look out at the town with a renewed interest.

I looked nothing like my sister and mother, other than sharing their eye color.

Where they had brunette hair, I had blonde hair with a slight curl at the ends, and baby blue eyes.

My skin was pale, unlike their sun-kissed skin.

I had always been a bit jealous of that, but no matter how much sun I had gotten, my skin wouldn't even begin to show a hint of a tan.

My mom had once told me that I looked a lot like my father, or sperm donor as she liked to put it. She had confessed to me that she had been raped when she conceived me. It had taken me a long time just to get that tiny bit of information from her. I thought that maybe if I knew more about him, then I would understand more about myself.

As you can imagine, it was a very touchy subject to bring up, so I never pushed her too hard, even though I was dying to learn more about who my father was.

"I haven't had the chance to meet them, but there might be." Mom answers Hannah's question.

I groan. "I think this is all going to blow up in our faces," I mutter before turning to the window to watch the town pass by.

"Nonsense, this will all work out, Piper; you'll see." Mom sing-songs her reply.

It made me want to gag. This would blow up in our faces, and they would be the ones to pay for my being… different.

"All I can see is us having to run, so no one throws me into a lab. I'm sorry, but I can't see any of this ending well, Mom." I answer honestly.

The rest of the ride goes by in complete silence, with everyone dwelling on my heavily weighted words.

It was one of our biggest fears, or at least mine.

If anyone were to discover my secret, I would be taken to some government lab and dissected like some animal.

I mean, how many humans out there could possibly have wings, and not just wings but could fly with those wings?

None, that's how many.

I was the only one of my kind. At least, that's what I had always thought. But maybe, there were others out there like me somewhere.

I could only hope.

As we pull up to a fancy white two-story house, I look questioningly at my mom.

We had never had a house this big or showy, and I was beginning to wonder what her plans were for this town.

My curiosity is only met with a quick wink before she exits the car. I watch as she signals to the moving truck that had been following us.

"Don't screw this up for us, Piper. Look how happy Mom is." Hannah clips out. "I want us to be able to stay here, and for once, I want to be able to have a steady boyfriend. Not just somebody I'm just going to have to leave behind again."

She exits the car, and I groan while placing my face into my hands.

As if I hadn't already felt bad enough, she had to go and bring up the past.

Hannah had made many great friends in the last town we lived in. She even had a really sweet boyfriend that would have done anything for her.

She blamed me for messing all of that up for her when Mom told us that we had to move, yet again.

In truth, it wasn't entirely my fault that we had to leave. I would have loved to stay in that town a while longer, but Mom didn't think like that idea. Well, until now, it seemed.

I wonder for a moment what could have changed her mind this time. What was her reason for wanting to stay in this particular town?

"This is going to be a nightmare." I sigh roughly before exiting the car.

As I shut the door, I glanced at the neighboring light grey-sided house that was just as large and grand as ours.

My eyes scan the windows before I spot a dark-haired man standing in the shadows, watching us. I could barely make him out other than the slight sparkle in his eyes from the sunlight.

I watch him as he watches us, and when his eyes meet mine, they darken while his lips turn into an angry frown.

I'm left puzzled as he disappears deeper into the shadows. I shrug it off when Mom passes me with her hands loaded with boxes.

"Go help your sister, Piper." She commands over her shoulder before entering the house.

I glance back at the window once more. Not seeing anything, I sigh and then walk over to the moving truck, where my sister is blatantly flirting with the moving men.

"Do you guys live around here?" She questions them while twirling a few strands of her hair around her finger.

The two men's eyes rake over my sister's well-formed and curvy body, and I roll my eyes.

Grabbing her arm, I force a smile while pointing at the two men sternly. "Hands off, boys, she's only sixteen."

Their eyes go wide before they rush off to lift the heavy boxes in the back of the truck.

Once they leave with their hands full, Hannah wrenches her arm from my grasp and then turns to glare at me with her hands on her hips.

"Why did you do that, Piper?" She demands.

I shrug and then plaster on a fake smile just to bug her.

"I hate you. I hate you for all of this, for us having to move all the time, for us not being able to have friends or even boyfriends. I wish you weren't my sister. I wish that bastard father of yours would come and take you away." She spits out harshly.

I back away from her as if slapped.

Some days I knew they secretly hated me, but to hear it said out loud breaks me.

I take a few more steps back as Mom returns to the truck.

She stops abruptly, glancing between us before her eyes settle on me. She must see the pain and sadness in my expression because her face softens as she takes a step toward me.

Instead of allowing her to comfort me, I back away with my hands up.

"What's wrong, Piper?" Mom asks softly.

I only shake my head as tears rapidly fill my eyes.

Her eyes quickly turn to Hannah, who is still staring daggers at me. "What did you say to her, Hannah?"

Hannah remains quiet.

"Someone answer me now." Mom demands.

When neither of us answers her, she throws her hands into the air in surrender.

"I hate you, Piper," Hannah bites out while still glaring at me.

Mom's jaw hits the ground as tears start running down my cheeks.

"Why would you say that to your sister, Hannah?" Mom questions in disbelief.

"Because it's true, Mom, I hate her, and I wish she would just disappear so we could have a normal life for once," Hannah answers her honestly.

My mom bows her head while pinching the bridge of her nose as she tries to reign in her anger.

"It's true, isn't it? You both want me gone, don't you?" I whimper.

When Mom's eyes turn to me with pity, my heart sinks. Whimpering again, I turn my back to them before I begin running.

I didn't know where to go, but I had to get away from them, if only for a little while.

"Piper, please come back so we can talk," Mom yells as I continue to run.

My feet hit the sidewalk with a smooth rhythm of thuds. With each beat, my body relaxes, and my emotions calm down.

I run until my legs feel like jelly before I slow to a walk while approaching a small empty playground.

Walking over to the swings absently, I sit down and begin to swing myself gently.

My mind rewinds to the words that my sister had said. It broke my heart to know that I was hurting them so much.

Why did I, of all people, have to end up being special? I didn't want this life.

Raven K. Asher

Leaning my head against the swing's chain, I gently swing myself while gazing up at the graying sky above me.

"Are you okay?" A soft squeaky voice asks while moving up beside me.

I glance over to a short girl with long brown hair and glasses. She flashes me a friendly smile while sitting on the swing next to me before she begins to swing.

"Yeah, I'm okay," I answer.

She nods and then begins to swing a little higher.

I watch her as she remains silent and closes her eyes before I turn my face back to look up into the sky once again.

"My name is Beth. What's yours?" She questions abruptly, breaking the silence.

Chuckling, I turn to look back at her. "I'm Piper."

"I like that name." She pauses for a moment. "So, I take it you've just moved here?"

"Yeah, I did, with my mom and my sister, Hannah," I answer quietly.

She stops swinging and watches me curiously for a few minutes.

"Are you sure there isn't something you want to talk about?" She asks softly. I shake my head in response, and she continues. "Well, if you ever want to talk, everyone always tells me I'm a good listener."

"Beth, I don't want to be mean or anything, but I'm not really looking for friends. I won't be around for long before we end up moving again." I reply gently.

Her lips form an 'o' while her eyes grow sad.

I instantly regret my words.

"That's okay. I don't have many friends anyway, but maybe I'll find some this year at school." She whispers sadly while bowing her head.

"You don't have any friends?" I ask while looking at her with surprise.

"No, I don't. Nobody really gives me a chance." She answers while glancing up at me from under her lashes.

"Well, you know what, I take back my comment. I guess I could use one good friend. I need someone who can guide me around the school. Would you be up for that?" I ask.

Her frown quickly turns into a grin, and before I know it, she slams into me. As she hugs me tightly, I awkwardly hug her back.

"Oh my God, thank you. You just totally made my day. I promise you won't regret this." She replies happily as she pulls back while bouncing on her feet.

I can't help but share some of her excitement.

Turning my face to the darkening sky, I groan.

I would have to start walking back now if I wanted to get back home before it became completely dark.

"I have to go, I've got a long walk home, and I want to beat the sunset," I state, causing Beth to bounce even more wildly on her feet.

"I can drive you." She exclaims excitedly.

"I mean, I can if you want me to, that is. I don't mind at all." She rambles, trying to calm herself down.

I chuckle and nod. "Alright, I'll let you drive me just this once, but next time I'll drive you, okay?"

She nods while biting down on her lip.

When she doesn't move, I wave my hand, allowing her to go first, and she jumps into action with a squeak.

I hold back my laughter.

Maybe having a friend like her wouldn't be so bad after all. No one had made me laugh this much in a very long time.

Once we're in her tiny blue VW Bug, I direct Beth back to my house.

She sings along to the songs on her radio as I stare out the window, wondering what I would say to my mother and sister.

I didn't know if I even wanted to face them, let alone talk to them.

"If you want to talk, I will listen, Piper. Whatever it is that's bothering you; I won't judge." Beth promises softly while turning the music off.

I turn to her, and for a moment, I find myself longing to tell her all of my problems.

Without warning, I let one slip.

"I had a fight with my sister…and she said some terrible things…." I trail off.

"Well, that is horrible." Beth huffs out dramatically.

I roll my eyes while letting out a laugh. "Yeah, she's sixteen and thinks she's the queen of the world."

"Well, then she would get along great with my sister, Sara," Beth answers with a sigh.

"If she's a mean girl, then yeah, they probably would," I reply, and Beth nods.

At least we had something in common.

"So, do you want to hang out tomorrow? I mean, if you're not doing anything else. You don't have to say yes if you don't want to." Beth rambles again, conveniently changing the subject.

I smile. "Yeah, we can hang out. Do you just want to meet somewhere?"

She shrugs. "Let me have your number, and I'll figure out a place that will be easy for you to find. Then we can make plans." She suggests. "Does that sound good?"

I nod. "Yeah, that sounds good."

She hands me her phone, and I quickly punch in my number before handing it back to her.

Pulling up to my house, she lets out a low whistle, and I look at her in question.

"You live here?" She asks, and I nod.

"Have you met your neighbors yet?" She then inquires while glancing towards the house beside mine.

"No, I haven't. Why?" I ask with a raised brow.

"From what I know of them, which isn't much, they're a very creepy bunch. There are four kids that live here, and all of them are strange, especially in school. They only ever talk to each other." She explains.

"That is weird. What else do you know about them?" I ask absently while turning my attention toward the neighbor's house.

"They are weird, but the one brother or whatever, Joel, he's been nice to me. He's the only one who has ever stuck up for me in school." She confesses quietly.

We stay quiet for a few moments, each of us lost in our own thoughts.

"You have me now, Beth," I assure her before quickly exiting the car.

Rushing to the door, I only glance back once her car leaves.

Taking a deep breath, I turn my attention back to the house. I mentally prepare myself for what was going to happen as soon as I opened the door.

I knew my mom would have a ton of questions for me to answer, and I didn't even know how I was going to answer them.

Taking breath after breath, I try to gather up the nerve to go in, but instead, I opt to sit out on the porch's white swing.

After only a few moments of swinging, my mom slowly and cautiously walks out to sit with me.

She stays silent for a few moments before grabbing my hand in hers. "I'm sorry about your sister, Piper. You know how she gets when we have to move."

I nod in understanding, and she continues. "I know saying sorry for her isn't going to fix things, but I want you to try. I want us to have a normal life here."

I nod again while looking out at the road.

"I saw a girl drop you off earlier. Did you make a friend?" She then asks with hope lacing her words.

"Yeah, I guess I did. She seems really nice, and she made me laugh." I whisper, knowing my mom would get the gravity of that.

She knew how sad and lonely I felt.

I couldn't help feeling like an outcast, and I hated getting close to people for fear of them stabbing me in the back.

It had happened far too many times to count.

"Am I going to get the chance to meet her?" Mom inquires next.

"Yeah, she wants to hang out tomorrow. I'll have her come by afterward." I reply with a nod.

And for once, it felt like I finally had a chance at a normal life.

"Good, I'm going to head back in." Mom sighs softly. "I've almost gotten the kitchen stuff unpacked, so we'll be able to have breakfast in the morning."

"That's great, Mom," I reply with a smile.

Grinning happily, she gives my hand one last squeeze before heading back inside.

I resume swinging and close my eyes as a slight breeze brushes through my hair.

After a little while, I shift around in discomfort. My back was beginning to hurt from keeping my wings hidden for so long.

Groaning, I bend over to relieve some of the pressure.

When it becomes too much, I rush inside and into the kitchen. My eyes widen when I realize there weren't any curtains up in the house yet.

"Mom, where are the curtains?" I state in a panic.

Her eyes go wide with sudden fear.

"I completely forgot. Oh god, what are we going to do?" She asks, panicked, as she begins dumping out boxes frantically.

Instead of waiting for her, I rush up the stairs before heading down the hall to a room I thought would be best hidden from view.

Mom follows me closely as I rush into the empty room and fall to my knees as I practically rip off my shirt.

"Are you going to be alright, Piper?" Mom questions quietly.

I nod while gritting my teeth in pain. "I'll be fine, Mom. I just held them in too long today."

She nods before leaving the room, shutting the door behind her.

I let another loud groan out as my wings slowly unfold from my back.

It was a relief to finally have them out. Moaning softly, I fan them, stretching them fully out in the room.

The breeze they create blows through my hair, and I close my eyes with a smile.

I wanted to go out for a flight, but it was too risky.

After a few calming moments, I open my eyes only to spot someone watching from a window in the neighboring house directly across from me.

A gasp falls from my lips as I back away into the shadows, praying that they hadn't seen my wings. I couldn't ruin things this fast.

It would suck if I had, especially considering we had just gotten here.

Kneeling on the floor, I continue to watch the shadow in the window.

I try my hardest to fold my wings away, but they refuse.

Without another option, I rise and then rush out into the hallway.

The only thing I could do was hold out hope that this situation wouldn't blow up just yet. For all I knew, they hadn't seen anything.

At least, that's all I could hope for.

"Mom, I need you here now," I yell.

Without hesitating, she rushes out of a room nearby.

I let out a deep breath realizing she had been hanging curtains in a room for me.

"I was just about to hang the curtains." She replies while holding up the dark fabric.

I smile but then point to the room behind me.

"Can I have that room as mine? My wings can really spread far in there." I ask softly.

She nods. "Sure, I'll be just a moment."

She moves into the room, and I watch from the doorway as she hangs the curtains.

Once they're up, I finally let out the breath I had been holding before walking back into the room.

Spreading my wings, I shiver as my mom gently runs her hands across the soft feathers.

"I always thought they were beautiful, Piper. But they've gotten so long…." She trails off as she steps in front of me.

"What's it feel like to fly?" She whispers curiously, surprising me.

I raise my brow in question. She had never asked me anything like that before.

"It's an amazing feeling. I'm completely free when I'm in the air; I feel whole." I answer truthfully.

She nods her head as her eyes stare off blankly at the wall.

After a minute of silence, she pats my shoulder and then makes her way out of the room.

Pausing, she glances back as she begins to shut the door. "I'll bring up some blankets. The movers didn't get everything moved in yet, but your bed should be here tomorrow."

I nod, and she closes the door.

Making my way over to the window again, I peek past the curtain and gasp before rubbing my eyes, thinking for sure that I had lost my mind because what I was seeing couldn't be real, or could it?

Through the shadows, I spot wings similar to my own. They were attached to the dark figure I had spotted earlier in the day.

I place my hand against the glass and watch in amazement as the figure does the same.

My door opening with a squeak startles me, and I quickly pull back, shutting the curtain as my mom struggles to come through the door with a pile of blankets in her arms.

I quickly move over to the door and take some of them from her hands before walking to the middle of the room, where I drop them to the floor.

"This is all I could find. I hope it will be enough." Mom states as she kneels and helps me form them into a bed on the floor.

"This should be fine, Mom," I reply with a smile.

When we're finished, I lie down, and she covers me up. I grin happily as she tucks me in before walking out of the room, shutting the light off before she shuts the door.

As I lay in my makeshift bed, I wonder if what I had seen had been real. Was it possible that I wasn't alone, that there were others out there like me, or was it all just my imagination getting the better of me?

As my eyes grow heavy, I drift off to sleep, dreaming of a world less lonely.

Chapter Two

The next morning, I groan while trying again to fold my wings away. Unfortunately, they refuse to meet my demands, so instead of forcing them, I throw on one of my shirts that my mom had specially made for when my wings were out.

It had buttons down the sides so I could snap it on and openings for the base of my wings to slip through.

It was a bit tricky to get on, but the shirt looked pretty cool once I did.

Heading downstairs, I peek around the corners, just in case.

Thankfully, I don't find anyone else home.

Searching the kitchen, I do come across a plate full of pancakes. I groan hungrily as I sit down and begin devouring them. They tasted like heaven.

Noticing a note on the side of the table a few minutes later, I pick it up and read it out loud. "Went to the store with Hannah. We will be back after noon. Love, Mom."

I sigh softly while laying the note back down before I return to my breakfast, finishing off the pancakes on my plate.

Once I'm done, I clean my dish and dry it, placing it back into the cabinet where it belongs before I turn and walk into the empty living room.

I spin around in a circle, not knowing what to do.

There was no way I could go outside in my current state, and there wasn't any furniture in the room either.

When someone knocks at the door, I stop dead in my tracks.

I look around the empty room for an answer, but when I realize how stupid I'm being, I roll my eyes at myself.

The knocking turns into pounding, and I cringe, hoping that whoever it was would just leave.

Unfortunately for me, they don't.

"Crap, now what am I supposed to do?" I whisper to myself and then roll my eyes again for talking to myself.

I had to be losing my mind.

With one more eye roll, I make my way over to the door and open it just enough that I could see out, but hopefully, whoever was on the other side wouldn't be able to see me.

"What the heck do you want?" I growl as the person on the other side nearly knocks the door loose from my hands as they hit it again.

"Oh, you're home." A man's voice states with surprise.

I open the door a little wider, and I'm met with a dazzling white smile, platinum blonde hair, and pale grey eyes.

"Yes, I am. Now, who are you, and what do you want?" I ask impatiently.

"My father wanted me to come over and greet our new neighbors. Do you mind if I come in?" He asks, and he pushes his way inside before I can answer.

I slam the door shut as he turns his back to me, all the while pleading silently for my wings to fold away.

Thankfully, they disappear seconds before he turns around to face me.

"Who do you think you are, just barging in like that?" I demand.

He chuckles and bows his head shyly.

"I'm Joel; I'm your neighbor." He laughs while pointing to himself.

I shake my head.

"Oh, ha, ha, funny man, now why did you barge in here like that?" I ask while folding my arms over my chest.

"I did it because I wanted to talk to you and because I knew you would just shut the door in my face." He confesses.

I drop my arms and bow my head while nodding in agreement. "You're right; I was thinking about it."

"So, what do you want to talk about?" I ask after a brief moment of silence.

He grins sheepishly.

"Honestly, I don't know; I didn't even think I'd get this far." He admits again with a snort of laughter.

I join him with a laugh.

"Well, could you give me a minute to change, and then we can talk somewhere where we can sit? You can think about what to say while I'm changing." I recommend.

"That will work." He replies while grinning brightly.

"Alright, I'll be right back," I state before running up the stairs quickly and into my room.

I practically rip off my shirt, thankful that my mom had made it where when my wings went away, the slits were covered with extra material.

I was going to have to thank her later.

After slipping on another form-fitting black low-cut tee, I head back down where Joel is still standing, looking lost and deep in thought.

"What are you thinking so hard about?" I question, startling him.

"It was nothing." He answers a bit bashfully.

I raise my brow in question but decide not to push.

"Let's go out on the porch; it's the only real place we can sit until the rest of our furniture arrives," I suggest as I wave him on and turn towards the door.

I turn back abruptly, and he slams into me, efficiently pinning me against the door.

His eyes widen.

"I didn't mean to do that. I'm sorry." He apologizes as his face turns a deep shade of red.

I breathe in deeply, and his scent, a unique mint with a hint of something unfamiliar, floods my senses.

He doesn't make a single move to get away from me.

"It's okay. It's my fault for turning without any warning." I whisper.

When his hands gently move to my hips, I shiver a little. His head then leans in towards mine, and I absently wet my lips.

"You're so beautiful." He whispers before his lips are suddenly pressed firmly against mine.

My mind screams for me to stop. I didn't even know this guy as we continue to kiss, but I couldn't seem to find the will to shove him away.

Finally, regaining control of my actions after a few minutes, I push Joel back.

We pant as we try to catch our breaths. His heated eyes meet mine. It was obvious that he hadn't wanted to stop.

The thing I do next, I blame on the complete loss of my mind and teenage hormones.

I rush him, knocking him to the floor as I press my lips back against his.

His arms wrap around me, and he laughs before flipping us, so I am now on the floor looking up at him with my own heated gaze.

"We should really stop." I pant out in between kisses.

He pulls back to search my eyes.

"We should, shouldn't we?" He laughs as his eyes sparkle with humor.

Again, he presses his lips to mine, and everything else around us fades away.

I swear I hear pounding in the background of my mind while we continue to kiss, but I block it out, not wanting to think about anything other than being with Joel.

"Joel, what the hell are you doing?" A voice suddenly growls out from above us.

Joel curses as he pulls back. His eyes close, and he leans down to whisper in my ear. "I'm sorry."

I'm startled when Joel is lifted off of me to his feet.

"Mason, it was nothing." Joel snarls while turning his attention to this newcomer.

"It didn't look like nothing from my point of view, Joel, and you know it," Mason growls as he grabs onto Joel's shirt, yanking him up into his dark face. "I told you to stay away from her."

Anger wells in my chest, and I jump to my feet before swiftly kicking Mason's legs out from under him.

His eyes go wide with shock, and his grip loosens on Joel as he falls to the floor with a hard thud.

I don't stop my assault as he lies motionless on the floor. Instead, I give a swift kick to his side and point my finger sternly at him.

"You're lucky that I only kicked your feet out from under you this time because I swear if you ever barge into my house again, I will kick you in the family jewels," I warn and then huff out a breath of air while placing my hands on my hips.

"What's your problem anyway?" I question roughly while staring down into the greenest eyes I had ever seen.

His jaw ticks in building anger while he flicks his head just enough to move his long shaggy hair from his eyes.

He growls before answering me. "You're my problem."

My jaw drops in disbelief.

I couldn't believe he had the audacity to say that.

"I'm your problem, really…? You just barged into my house and yelled at me, and I'm your problem?" I practically shout.

"Come on, guys. Let's stop this now before it gets any worse." Joel pleads while grabbing my waist to pull me away from Mason.

Mason stands to his feet, and Joel pulls me back, trying to diffuse the situation.

With a hoarse laugh, Mason shakes his head as he watches us closely. His hand points to Joel behind me, and Joel stops.

"At least tell me you got her name before you kissed her, Brother." Mason laughs in amusement while Joel curses behind me.

"You didn't, did you?" He laughs again.

Growing angry again, I rush forward, pulling out of Joel's grasp.

My hand cracks loudly against his face, effectively erasing his cocky smirk.

"Get out of my house, now." I then demand.

He pins me with a glare.

"You heard her, Joel; leave now." He then growls, his eyes never leaving mine.

"I meant you," I shout louder while getting into his face.

From the corner of my eye, I spot Joel leaving the house with his head bowed. The sight only fuels my building anger further.

I shove my hands against Mason's hard chest and shriek in anger. "Get out."

"I'm not leaving until you, and I come to an understanding first." He snarls while stepping forward.

I take steps back until my back hits a wall. I curse at my stupidity and then prepare for the harsh words I am sure would come out of his mouth.

He moves so close that his toes touch mine. For a moment, his eyes soften, and I swear he leans in like he's going to kiss me, just like Joel had, but instead of making a move, he shakes his head hard.

His eyes grow hard again, and I shiver in fear as the green of his eyes fades to almost black.

"I don't ever want you around my brother again. I don't want to even see you or hear about you. If you were smart, you'd leave this town now. Do you hear me?" He bites out as his hand slams against the wall beside my head, causing me to jump.

I nod as tears build in my eyes.

"I was going to leave anyway, but alone. Leave my sister and mother out of this, whatever it is. Your problem is only with me." I reply.

His eyes soften as he studies me for a few moments.

He then nods and then leaves the house just as quickly as he had come.

I slide down the wall onto my butt.

When my phone rings a few moments later, I glance down at the screen to see Beth calling. I hit the ignore button and close my eyes.

I should have known that I wouldn't be welcome here, and I should have known that I was never going to get a chance at true happiness.

I don't know how much time goes by, but I stay seated on the floor as the movers begin moving our furniture in. They don't even glance at me as they walk past, and once again, deep loneliness creeps into my heart.

A little while later, I stand abruptly and rush out of the house, needing to get away. I run past my mom, Hannah, and Beth as I make my way over to my beautiful black bike that had finally arrived.

"Wear your helmet, Piper," Mom yells out quickly.

I turn in her direction as she throws me my helmet. I catch it and then slip it over my hair. Then, as Beth comes over to me, I flip up the visor.

"Why didn't you answer your phone when I called?" She asks softly.

I take a deep breath to prepare myself for the harsh words I need to say. I didn't want to hurt her, but it was for the best.

"I really don't want to be your friend, Beth. Just leave me alone," I growl out simply before throwing my leg over the bike, ending the conversation before she could say another word.

I turn it on and close my eyes as the hum of the engine fills me with happiness.

Riding it was almost as freeing as flying.

"Why?" Beth whimpers, breaking into my thoughts.

I bow my head, not wanting to look at her as she begins to cry beside me, whimpering just loud enough to be heard over the bike's engine.

I didn't want to feel bad for making her cry, so I do the only thing I knew how. I flip my visor down and back the bike up so I can ride away.

Even though I didn't want to look back at Beth, some unknown force makes me.

I'm relieved when I spot Joel walking over to her. At least not everyone would be as mean to her as I had just been.

My eyes then scan over to Mason, who was watching me from his porch.

I rev the bike's engine, taking off as I flip him my middle finger. As I ride down the street, I swear I see him chuckling in my mirrors.

Honestly, I didn't know what to make of him. I couldn't help but wonder if he really was a jerk or if there was something more to him.

Going through town, I take reckless turns while pushing my bike well past average speeds. I didn't fear what could happen if I were to wreck. I had found out a long time ago that I could survive the worst when I had decided to jump out of a four-story apartment window.

While I had broken many of my bones, they healed within weeks.

Everyone had said I shouldn't have been able to survive a fall like that, but I had.

Riding around aimlessly, I move through the town, getting a feel for the area. I also needed to find a place where I could fly safely and not be seen.

With a bit of luck, I find a small secluded patch of forest not far from the town. I park my bike nearby and then sit on a bench in a small clearing beside the forest.

I sit there enjoying the peace and quiet until a presence joins me.

Looking back, I groan when I see Joel.

"You're not supposed to be around me," I scold while turning back around to look into the forest surrounding the clearing blankly.

He sits down next to me, resting his elbows on his knees. "I don't always do as I'm told."

"Well, your brother is right to warn you away from me. I'm no good for anyone," I reply.

"I don't think that's true." He argues lightly.

I shake my head. "Joel, you don't even know my name, and we kissed, and it wasn't just a small kiss; it was…well, you know."

I glance over at him as a smirk crosses his lips.

"I agree, it wasn't small, but it was amazing. You're right, though; I should have asked your name first." He replies.

I nod my head in agreement and then turn my attention back out toward the swaying trees for a few moments before looking back at Joel.

"How about we just start over?" I suggest abruptly.

He grunts in agreement and then thrusts his hand in my direction.

I laugh as I slip my hand into his.

"Hi, I'm Joel." He laughs as we shake.

"Hello, I'm Piper," I reply with a grin.

His eyes sparkle as he tries to hold in his laughter.

"I like that name." He then whispers before releasing my hand.

"Thanks," I whisper back as I scoot closer to him absently before laying my head against his shoulder.

"We can't let your brother know about this." I then plead.

"I won't say a word." He replies quietly.

"Good." I sigh.

We sit quietly as the sky darkens and the moon shines down on us.

For the first time in a very long time, I finally felt comfortable with someone and didn't feel quite as lonely.

It was a good feeling, but one that I knew wouldn't last.

Even as tears fill my eyes and spill down my cheeks, not a word is spoken between us. Instead, Joel just silently wipes them away as he holds onto me.

When they finally stop, Joel kisses the top of my head before standing to his feet and walking away.

I listen and wait until his footsteps fade into the distance.

As soon he's gone, I stand to my feet and walk towards the trees, glancing around just in case before stepping into the darkness.

Once I'm in the woods deep enough, I pull off my shirt and tuck it tightly into my back pocket before rubbing my arms against the chill in the air.

I look around at my surroundings once more before I sigh and then allow my wings to unfold.

A soft moan leaves my lips as they stretch and flap gently behind me.

Smiling, I gaze toward the sky before I push off the ground.

I fly up and above the trees.

The air caresses my skin as I twist and turn. I soar higher and higher, reaching for that feeling of freedom I longed for so badly.

After twenty minutes, exhaustion sets in. I reluctantly fly back down to the ground and fold my wings back away before sliding my shirt back on while heading back out of the woods.

Walking over to my bike, I get the strange sensation of someone watching me, but when I scan around the clearing, I don't spot anything or anyone.

I shrug the feeling off and mount my bike before sliding my helmet on.

I rub my arms for a moment, wishing that I had brought my jacket with me before taking off on my bike to go back home.

Chapter Three

Walking into the kitchen the next morning, I'm surprised to see my sister sitting at the table with three new friends, one of whom looked much like Beth.

"Good morning, Piper." Mom greets happily as she carries a plate of fresh-cut fruit over to the girls.

I grin and walk over to the counter, where she had a plate of pancakes stacked for me.

The smell of blueberries floating up from the stack was heavenly. I breathe the scent in deeply while closing my eyes.

After a moment, I open my eyes and then sit at the counter bar before taking my first delicious bite.

"Are you girls getting excited about school tomorrow?" Mom asks abruptly.

The girls at the table instantly begin talking wildly at the same time while letting out little squeals of excitement.

I groan inwardly and roll my eyes.

"I'm not ready," I answer.

This time it's my mom's turn to roll her eyes. She knew how much I hated school.

"You're never ready, Piper." She answers while leaning her hip against the counter.

"That's because I never make any friends, Mom. You know it's never been easy for me." I reply around a mouthful of pancake.

Her eyes scan me for a minute as she decides what to say next.

"I thought you were making friends. I came home to two guys coming out of the house, for goodness sake, and before I forget, what was that about anyway?" She questions while pinning me with a look.

I gulp and swallow my food before searching for a response.

"They were just being neighborly?" I answer her with another question.

Not my smoothest move, but it was all I could come up with.

She rolls her eyes, not believing a word. "Sure... I was young once, you know, and you can't exactly erase that just kissed look, Piper." She laughs while placing her hand on my shoulder.

"I don't even know why I kissed him back. I didn't even know him." I whisper. "It won't happen again, though. You missed one heck of a fight that I had with his brother. That's why they were both here."

She sighs. "Just be careful, whatever you do, Piper. I know I can't stop you, but promise me that you'll be careful."

"I will, Mom," I promise before taking another bite of my breakfast.

I continue to eat silently until my plate is clean.

Mom takes it from my hands, and I smile gratefully before returning to my room.

I shut and then lock my door to stop anyone from accidentally coming in. Walking over to my pile of boxes, I begin the daunting task of finding a place for everything.

I grin as I pull out the large black wings my mom had made me years ago. We had used them many times as an excuse for why people had seen me with wings.

For those reasons, I was thankful that my mom was very talented and artistic.

After hanging them on the wall above my bed, I place my collection of bird photographs I had taken on another wall.

Each one had its own special meaning. Each bird held a memory of a moment when I had found a tiny bit of happiness.

I had them to remind myself that not all things were bad.

Next, is my collection of books. I run my fingers along their covers as I place each one lovingly onto my bookshelves.

Again, they all had special meaning, especially the ones about angels. They gave me a world where I felt like I actually belonged.

After placing everything in its place and unpacking my clothes, I lie back on my bed and stare at my ceiling. I was going to have to do something with it.

I was not too fond of a dull white ceiling.

"Hey, Piper, can I come in for a second?" Hannah asks while knocking on my door.

I groan softly but get up to open it for her while wondering if she was coming to apologize. That would be unusual for my sister to do, though, so there had to be another reason that she wanted to talk.

I open the door just a sliver, but instead of my sister on the other side Joel pushes his way in and then locks my door behind him.

"What are you doing?" I question while placing my hand on my hip.

He smiles and motions back at the door absently. "Do you know that your sister is quite the trickster?" I nod, and he continues. "I had to bribe my way in here; it cost me a kiss and fifty bucks."

I shake my head and laugh as I walk over to my bed.

I sit down and smirk up at him. "You're just giving away your kisses right and left these days, Joel."

"Yeah, I know. I feel dirty after that kiss. She's a bit of a wildcat, that one." He laughs while pointing to the door again as he shakes his head. "I barely got away from her."

"Why are you here?" I ask, wanting to change the subject.

"Oh, I just wanted to see if you were alright." He answers, becoming serious.

"I am." I breathe out while lying back on the bed.

"Are you sure? You still seem… sad?" He questions gently before sitting on the edge of my bed while looking down at me.

"I am, I promise," I insist, watching as his eyes travel to the wings hanging on the wall above us.

"Those are pretty cool. Did you make them yourself?" He questions.

I shake my head. "No, my mom did. She's pretty talented."

"Yes, she is." He agrees.

A few moments of awkward silence go by before he speaks again. "Are you ready for school tomorrow?"

"No, I'm not looking forward to it at all," I answer honestly.

"Why aren't you?" He asks curiously.

Instead of answering him, I avoid the question with my own question.

"Are you?" I ask while raising my brow.

He nods. "Well, I guess I am, but don't turn this back on me. Why aren't you looking forward to it? Aren't you excited to make new friends and all that?"

"Joel, I don't make friends. What I do make is enemies with every girl out there, and I don't know why but no matter how hard I try, the girls hate me, and the guys… well, the guys just get stupid around me." I answer truthfully.

"Really…?" He replies in disbelief.

I nod. "Yes, it's crazy, right? You're honestly the first guy that I've encountered that I can actually talk to normally."

"Yeah, but you forget that I did act a little odd when we first met." Joel snorts.

"True, but now things are better, and that's got to mean something, right?" I insist.

He nods his head in agreement. "You were able to talk to Beth, too."

"She would make a good friend, you know. She needs friends around her. I can't always be there to stand up for her." He adds.

"I don't know if she'll even want to talk to me now. I was pretty mean to her yesterday." I confess.

"She understands what happened. I talked to her. She'll give you another chance, I promise." He assures.

"Thanks, Joel, for everything," I reply softly before covering my eyes with my arm, trying to hide my face.

"No problem, Piper." He answers before lying down next to me.

Once again, a comfortable silence takes over.

His hand slides into mine, and once again, I found myself feeling a little less lonely.

After what feels like hours pass, he moves to get to his feet. Instead of letting him leave, I hold his hand, forcing him to stay in a sitting position as I sit up next to him.

I lean in and gently kiss his lips.

"Thank you," I whisper, kissing him once more before finally letting him stand.

He grins mischievously and pulls me up to him before kissing me senseless.

Pulling back, his eyes search mine for a moment.

"Thank you, Piper." He pants and then releases me before quickly leaving my room without another word.

I touch my fingers to my lips and smile. Maybe I'd have the chance to have a real relationship after all.

"Piper, who was that boy in your room with you?" My mom interrupts my thoughts as she marches in.

"That was Joel, and he just wanted to talk. He was worried about me after yesterday." I answer honestly, surprising myself.

I hadn't been this honest in, well… forever.

"He seemed nice." She replies with a smile as she sits down with me on my bed.

I nod my head in agreement.

"Are you being careful?" She inquires seriously, causing my jaw to drop.

My mind screams. Oh god, I so did not need *the* talk.

"Mom, I barely know him, and if I were going to do that, I would be careful. However, you don't have to worry because that will not happen anytime soon." I practically squeak out.

I wasn't exactly a good girl. I had kissed guys and had fooled around a little, but it never went as far as what she was insinuating.

Let the record show; I was still a virgin and proud to be one.

"Oh, so your still…?" She trails off, and I nod.

"Yes, Mom, I am, but am I really the one you should be worried about? Joel told me that Hannah made him kiss her to get in here. He even had to pay her." I laugh.

Mom grits her teeth together before she sighs roughly. "I probably should talk to her. She will be the death of me."

I snort and nod my head in agreement.

"You're a good girl, Piper. Don't let anyone take advantage of you; wait for that right one to come along." She adds.

"I will, Mom," I promise.

Standing up, she leans down to kiss my cheek before leaving my room.

I laugh a few minutes later when Hannah squeals loudly in the hallway and then begins yelling at my mom about not needing the talk.

Her anger quickly switches to me, and I stand up and walk over to the door to listen.

"Why is Piper allowed to have boys in her room?" She whines.

"Because I can trust her, I can't trust you, Hannah," Mom yells.

"Piper always gets her way; we do everything for Piper. It's always about Piper. When is it going to be about what I want?" Hannah whines again.

"You know why we do what we do for Piper. We protect her. If you think that this life is easy for her, you're dead wrong, Missy. Piper is always going to have to live in fear. She will have to move over and over while you and I will finally be able to settle down. At any moment, she could be taken away from us, and trust me, if that happens, you will feel sorry, and you will regret being so mean to her."

"I hate her, Mom, and I hate you," Hannah yells abruptly and then runs into her room, slamming the door.

I watch from my doorway as Mom's shoulder slump. I realize then that she had carried around just as much fear as I had.

She wipes her eyes as she cries silently.

I open my door, and she looks at me sadly. Then, without hesitating, I rush over to her with my arms held out for a hug. I embrace her tightly as she begins to sob into my shoulder.

"I'm so sorry, Mom." I cry with her.

She shakes her head. "Don't be sorry, Baby. I love you. I'm just so afraid of losing you."

"You're never going to lose me, Mom, never," I promise confidently.

Her hand comes up to cup my cheek. "I hope not."

She straightens her shoulders a few seconds later and then wipes her eyes as she forces a smile. "Are you hungry?"

I nod. "Yeah, I am, Mom."

She nods and then walks away.

I watch as she disappears down the stairs before I fall to my knees as a sharp wave of pain washes through me without warning, causing my wings to shoot out from my back.

A strangled scream falls from my lips as the pain quickly becomes overwhelming. It felt as if every cell in my body was exploding.

Hannah runs out of her room before kneeling next to me as I continue to cry out in pain.

Mom is next to come running back up the stairs.

Fear washes over me as I realize where we are. I was in the hall with my wings exposed, and that Hannah had friends over.

"Hannah, are your friends still here?" I pant out.

She thankfully shakes her head.

"They left a while ago." She replies before I let out another loud scream.

"What's wrong, Piper?" Mom cries out frantically.

My only response is to scream again.

"My wings, they feel like they're on fire." I cry.

Mom panics, but there isn't anything we can do.

"What are we going to do, Mom? We can't call for help. What do we do?" Hannah begins sobbing.

"I don't know, Sweetheart, I don't know." Mom sobs with her.

Mom touches my wings gently before letting out a scream of panic as she pulls her hand away. I begin to sob when I see her hand covered in blood.

"Oh, God, what's wrong with me?" I cry.

She shakes her head, unable to form words.

"I have to call for help, Piper. We don't have any other choice." Hannah cries.

I shake my head. "No, Hannah, what they would do to me would be much worse than this."

Suddenly, without warning, a bright flash of light engulfs the hallway, startling us.

A man appears, and my mom curses as she stands to her feet, placing herself between him and me.

"What are you doing here, Michael?" She growls.

"I must help Helen, or she will die." The man replies calmly while nodding in my direction.

Mom glances back at me and then back to him before moving out of his way.

Kneeling next to me, he places his fingers under my chin, so I have no choice but to look up at him.

He looked so much like me, with his long blonde curly hair and blue eyes. Even his black wings were similar to mine.

"Piper, I know this will be hard to understand, but I'm your father, and I'm here to help you. I can take away the pain, but you must do something for me, understand?" He asks calmly.

I blink a few times as my vision blurs while I try my hardest to understand what is going on.

After a moment, I answer him. "Yes."

He grins. "That's my girl."

"I need to get my blood inside you. I know that it sounds gross, but it will be the only way to keep you alive." He explains gently.

I then watch as he cuts his wrist open with a silver knife.

He holds it to my mouth and raises his brows. "Drink now, Daughter."

My eyes widen as I shake my head and back away from him.

"You have to." He almost pleads.

Again, I shake my head.

He looks to my mother for help. She nods once before moving closer. She then grabs my head as Hannah grabs my arms.

"You can't make me," I scream, even though I knew they intended to feed me his blood whether I liked it or not.

They would have done anything to keep me safe and alive.

My father pulls me up so I'm standing and then moves behind me while holding my wings tightly to my body.

He forces his wrist into my mouth, and I cry as the warm coppery liquid flows down my throat.

I struggle hard to get away from them but fail.

I couldn't beat all three of them.

After a few minutes, the pain begins to dull, and I give in, slumping back against my father's chest as he chants unknown words into my ear.

They comfort me a little as my eyes flutter and then close.

"Is she going to be alright now?" Mom questions softly as my eyes fight to stay open.

"Yes, but she's going to need me around for a while until we can be sure that she won't have any more of these spells. It's possible since she's one of a kind." Michael responds.

"What do you mean, Michael?" Mom asks quietly.

Unfortunately, before I can hear his answer, my world goes black, and I fall into a swirling pit of darkness.

Chapter Four

I wake up in my room alone, and for a minute, I think that maybe everything that had happened had been a dream, but as I touch my wings, the dried blood coating them flakes away under my fingertips.

Unfortunately, it had been real.

Groaning, I stand to my feet before trying to fold my wings away. To make things worse, they don't respond to my demands.

I couldn't even make them flap.

Quickly finding one of my unique shirts, I rush to snap it into place before heading downstairs, where I thankfully find my mom and Michael talking together while sitting at the kitchen table.

They both turn their attention toward me when I enter.

Mom stands to her feet and quickly grabs me in a hug.

"We have a lot to talk about, Piper." She whispers before pulling me to sit down across for Michael. "For starters, I want you to officially meet your father, Michael."

He smiles and holds out his hand, but I just glare at him in anger.

"My father, huh? I think not. If he were really my father, then he wouldn't have left me to live like this, thinking that I was all alone." I growl out harshly.

He bows his head and closes his eyes before pinching the bridge of his nose.

After a moment, he opens his eyes to look at me again while sighing roughly. "I didn't even know I had a daughter until yesterday. So, when I felt your pain, it took me by complete surprise."

My anger quickly disappears. I could clearly see in his eyes that he was telling the truth.

"How did you not know?" I question curiously.

He shakes his head and shrugs. "Our kind can't have daughters, and we keep track of when we have sons."

"I only have one. I'm very careful." He adds.

"What is our kind exactly?" I ask quietly, unsure if I wanted to really know.

"I am a fallen dark, purebred angel, which makes you, since your mother is human, the first ever dark Nephilim female." He answers.

My eyes go wide as I take in a sharp breath.

It was like a scene right out of one of my books.

"How did that happen? What does that mean for me, and why did it have to happen to me?" I fire off question after question.

He holds up his hand to stop me while laughing in amusement. "You're definitely my daughter. You ask too many questions, just like your brother does."

"Who's my brother?" I ask next curiously.

"His name is Cameron, and he will be here tomorrow. He's going to teach you a lot of things about what we are and to protect you while I'm away. He will also be able to help you if what happened yesterday happens again." He explains easily.

"Where's Hannah?" I ask, suddenly turning towards my mother, realizing she isn't here.

"She's in her room. She's very worried about you." Mom answers.

"Can you go get her and bring her down?" I request.

"I can do that." She agrees with a nod before standing and walking away.

"I'm sorry I haven't been here for you, Piper." Michael begins after she leaves.

I stop him by raising my hand. "Don't be sorry; you're here now. I need to know that you're not just going to leave us alone, though. I need you, and my mom needs you. This whole ordeal has been hell for us. We've had to move and hide for years. So, you have to promise that you will protect them too."

He nods. "I will, Piper. I promise I'm not going anywhere now. I vowed to love my kids with all of my heart, and I will make this up to you and your mom, but I'll warn you now that we may have to leave them if I find out you're in danger, being what you are."

"That's fine. Just keep them safe no matter what." I stress.

He nods with a growing grin on his face as he reaches his hand up to caress the side of my face in a fatherly way.

"Are you still tired?" He asks, and I shake my head no. "Good. Do you think you can handle going to school today?"

"I think so, but only if my wings decide to cooperate. They won't move for me at all," I answer.

His brows scrunch together before he directs me to stand.

I turn around and close my eyes as his hands roam over them.

"I don't see anything wrong other than the blood. That might be why they won't work. They can sometimes have a mind of their own." He explains as I turn around to face him once more.

"So, what, shower and see how they feel then?" I ask, and he nods.

I sit down but stand again when my sister rushes over to me. I hug her tightly as she cries.

"I'm so sorry, Piper. I shouldn't have been so mean." She apologizes.

"It's alright, Hannah. I'm fine now, and soon everything will be better," I assure her.

When her sobs finally ease up a few moments later, I push her back to look into her red-ringed eyes. "I will be fine," I promise again.

She nods her head while wiping away the tears staining her cheeks.

"Now, go get yourself pretty before we have to go to school." I then command lightly with a smile.

She wordlessly nods again before rushing back out of the room.

Mom walks back into the kitchen, smiling before sitting beside Michael.

I watch them for a moment before sighing. "I'm going to go shower."

Heading upstairs slowly, I grab my stuff from my room to shower with and then move off to the bathroom down the hall.

Stripping down quickly, I enter the shower.

The warm water washes over my wings, soothing them as I moan out in pleasure.

I cringe when I glance down to see all the blood pouring off them.

"At least they don't hurt anymore," I whisper as I soap them and wash all the blood out of the feathers.

When I finish, I towel dry off as much as possible before awkwardly wrapping the towel around myself, so I could go into my room to spread my wings.

I stumble to a stop when I reach my door, spotting a younger version of Michael with much shorter cut hair sitting on my bed.

Placing my hand on my hip, I cock my eyebrow.

"You must be Cameron?" I ask, and he nods as a mischievous grin crosses his lips.

He stands to his feet. "Yes, but you can just call me Cam."

"Can you leave?" I ask a bit rudely.

He shakes his head. "No, Dad wants me to check your wings and make sure you can hide them away."

I growl and slam the door shut.

"Fine, but just remember you're my brother." I clip out.

He holds up his hands as he laughs. "I'm only a half-brother."

I throw my towel at him before I quickly rush to my dresser and slide on panties, a bra, and a pair of jeans.

Turning back to face Cam, I let out a sigh of relief. He was thankfully turned the other way.

"You can turn around now." I laugh.

He does while peeking through his fingers.

73

"Oh, thank God." He sighs. "I was just joking before, you know. I never want to see my sister naked."

"I was hoping you were, but you never know these days." I chuckle.

He laughs with a nod of agreement.

"Well, Sis, let's see if those wings of yours are going to listen to you." He states, growing serious as he motions for me to move them.

Nodding, I stretch them out. This time they respond.

Flapping them a few times, I allow the air to dry them.

I let out a breath of relief that they were finally reacting to my commands, but when I try to hide them, they don't budge.

"They won't hide." I groan in disappointment.

"Turn back around; maybe we've missed something." He breathes out while directing me to turn my back to him.

I turn quickly while watching him over my shoulder.

"Sometimes, during the change you went through last night, they can get a little fractured, making it hard for them to function properly. I need to check them, but if I find a fracture, I hate to say this, but I'll have to break it in order to fix it. It will be excruciating." Cam explains gently.

I nod and stand patiently as his fingers begin to brush over every inch of my wings. When his fingers hit a particular tender spot, I cry out while falling to my knees.

"That hurt really bad right there." I pant out.

He moves to kneel next to me. "I have to fix that, and it will be the worst pain because it's such a major part of your wing structure." He states softly. "I need to get our father for this because I'm going to need someone to hold you steady."

I nod, and he quickly moves away before rushing out of my room. He returns moments later with our father.

Michael helps me back to my feet.

"Cam, is that the only fracture you found?" He questions.

"I still have the other wing to check, but I think that's it for the first," Cam answers him.

"Check the rest, and then we'll do the breaks all at once, so it's not as hard on her," Michael orders gently.

Cam nods before moving behind me as our father hugs my body tightly against his.

As Cam hits another sore spot, I cry out and bury my face into Michael's chest.

He rubs my arms soothingly. "Shhhh, Sweetheart, it will all be better soon, I promise."

"I'm almost done, Sis." Cam chimes in.

I nod and shut my eyes tightly.

After two more tender spots, I sway as Michael steps back.

His hands hold my arms while his eyes search mine. "Are you going to be alright?" He asks.

I shake my head. "It hurts too much, and you haven't even begun to fix them," I whisper.

He looks over my shoulder to Cam with a raised brow.

"She has six different major fractures." Cam sighs. "I wish that I had better news. It's more than likely going to cause her to pass out, but in a way that would be better for her, at least."

I cringe at Cam's words as tears begin to fall from my eyes.

"Don't cry, Piper. Please, don't cry." Michael begs softly as his thumbs wipe away my tears.

"I need my mom; please get her for me," I whisper.

He nods before walking away.

As I sway again, Cam catches me this time before I hit the ground.

"Just pass out now if you can, Sis. I'm sorry that I'm going to have to hurt you. Please forgive me." He whispers in my ear before his hand hits a tender spot before he twists it so it breaks.

I cry out and fall to my knees.

He quickly cracks another and then another as my mom and Michael rush back in.

"You should have waited, Cam," Michael growls out angrily.

I look up at them as tears continue to fall down my cheeks.

"I didn't want you to see this, Dad. I didn't want you to have to see her cry." Cam replies before breaking another fracture.

I cry out, and my mom falls to her knees in front of me. I bury my face in her shoulder as she wraps her arms around me.

While gritting my teeth against the pain, Cam makes the final breaks.

I fall back into his arms when he's done, feeling completely numb.

"Drink, Sis." He then commands as his wrist hovers over my mouth.

Without caring like I had before, I open my mouth for him as he places it against my lips. The blood flows down my throat, and I groan softly.

Glancing up, I see Michael holding onto my mom. Watching them together like that made me thankful that he had finally come back. She needed his support.

Cam pulls his arm away, and I turn my head to him as he looks up to see our parents.

A smile crosses his lips as he glances back down at me.

"Can you carry me to my bed, Cam?" I ask.

"I can do that." He replies with a nod before easily picking me up. He then moves over to my bed and tenderly places me down, so my wings are off to the side.

He sits beside me and shakes his head while looking at me in awe. "How are you still awake? I would have easily passed out after the first two breaks. I could never have made it through all six."

"I'm one tough cookie." I laugh.

"Yes, you are, Sis." He agrees with a laugh of his own.

After a few moments, I grab his hand to gain his full attention.

"Thank you," I whisper.

He nods, knowing precisely what I was thanking him for. If I had been in his position, I would have done the same thing in order to spare our parents the pain of seeing their kid so helpless.

"You would do it for me, right?" He inquires.

I nod. "Of course, I would."

"Good." He replies with a gentle smile.

Hannah comes in after a while but remains standing by the doorway. "We only have twenty minutes until we have to leave for school."

I nod, and Cam stands to his feet. "We better get ready then." He states as he holds his hand out to me.

Placing my hand in his, I allow him to pull me up to stand next to him.

I sway a little before he wraps his arm around my waist to keep me steady.

"Try your wings out, Piper, see if they feel better," Michael suggests gently while moving to stand in front of me.

Stretching them, I smile, feeling the difference. After flapping them back and forth a few times, I close my eyes and silently pray for them to go away.

When I reopen my eyes, Michael claps his hands together once with joy.

"Good job, Sis." Cam praises.

I turn to smile at him. "They felt a ton better, and the motion was a lot smoother," I reply while rubbing my arms, still feeling weakened.

"Good. Hopefully, next time this happens, it won't be as bad," Michael whispers.

We all nod in agreement.

"Well, let's get you dressed and ready for school, shall we?" Cam insists while moving me over to the edge of my bed to sit.

Mom jumps into action, grabbing a shirt from my dresser before handing it to Cam. He slides it over my head and then helps me push my arms through.

I was still beyond exhausted.

"I don't know how well this is going to go today. I can barely function." I whisper.

Cam smirks. "Well, then, it's a good thing I have every one of your classes. I'll carry you through them all if I have to."

"Why am I not surprised?" I snort loudly as I run my fingers through my hair.

"You don't have to go if you don't want to, Piper." My mom states supportively.

I shake my head. "I'll be fine, Mom."

With Cam's help, I could tough through my first day.

A few moments later, Cam helps me downstairs. As we head to the front door, I stop him. He turns to look at me in question, and I shake my head.

"I can't have you carrying me everywhere, Cam. People are going to wonder what's wrong with me." I sigh before continuing. "I think the best we can do is allow me to walk on my own as much as possible. You can pretend to be my boyfriend at school and hold me up by my waist if I need help." I suggest, and he nods with a smile.

"Fine by me, but I want to break up when this is over." He jokes lightly.

I laugh with him and shake my head. "You're a real comedian."

As our laughter dies down, we walk outside together, but before we get far, he comes to a complete stop as he glances around at the driveway.

My sister passes by us and then jumps into her car before driving off.

Cam looks at me with a raised brow before I hand over my keys to the bike.

I didn't have a car.

He looks around again, then back to me in question.

"Where's your car?" He asks.

I wordlessly point toward the bike.

His eyes widen before his mouth forms a boyish grin. "I get to drive that?"

"Yeah, but you have to be careful with my baby," I command sternly.

He nods as we walk over to it.

Trailing his hand over the sleek black metal, he lets out a low whistle of appreciation before he hops onto it and hands me my helmet.

I hesitate a moment, wondering if he had ever even driven a motorcycle.

He must see the question in my eyes because he shakes his head. "Don't worry, Sis, I have one of these back home. I just never thought that you, a girl, would have one."

My lips form an 'o' before I smile and slide my helmet on.

I mount the back of the bike but groan as the helmet hits Cam's back.

Sliding it back off, I throw it to Michael, who was watching us from the porch. He catches it and then waves goodbye to us while Cam begins backing us down the driveway.

Just as we pull into the road, I turn my head to see Joel, Mason, and two girls come out of their house.

Joel smiles at me, but it quickly turns into a frown when he spots Cam. With a soft sigh, I wrap my arms around Cam's waist, causing him to chuckle.

"Are you trying to make them jealous, Piper?" He whispers.

I pinch him, and he yelps.

"Yep, I guess so." He then laughs before revving the bike's engine. "Let's make some boys jealous, then." He teases while placing his hand over mine, holding onto me tightly as he forces the bike onto its rear tire to pop-a-wheelie.

I squeal with laughter as we speed off down the road before the front tire returns to the pavement.

Glancing back, I see Joel still frowning and Mason standing next to him with a matching frown.

I was never going to understand him.

****

Cam and I end up taking the long way to get to school.

I bark out in laughter when we pull up next to Joel and Mason in the parking lot. I smack Cam's back, and he shrugs, acting all innocent.

He holds my hand tightly as I get off the bike and follows suit. I sway a little, and his arm quickly wraps around my waist to hold me steady.

"Hey, guys." Cam greets, waving toward Mason and Joel.

I turn my head to his side to hide my chuckle.

"Hey, are you from around here?" Mason questions while walking over to us.

Quickly becoming serious, I wrap my arms around Cam's waist.

"Just moved in with my dad, who's dating Piper's mom," Cam answers easily.

Joel stands up next to Mason, his jaw ticking with anger. "Are you two dating now or something?" He questions while pinning me with a look.

I shrug. "What does it matter to you?"

He takes a step back, looking wounded, before he throws his hands into the air in surrender. Then, without saying a word, he rushes off toward the school.

Mason steps up closer to us and gives me a cruel grin. "I know you and Joel have been meeting up privately even though I warned you not to. I don't know what you're doing with this joke, but don't hurt my brother."

Stepping away from Cam, I poke my finger into Mason's chest in anger. "You told me to stay away, and I did. He came to me. If you want him to stay away, he has to believe that Cam is my boyfriend."

Taking a step back, I sway a little before Mason grabs my arm to keep me steady as he glances between Cam and me.

"So, you two aren't really dating?" He questions with a raised brow.

I laugh harshly and shake my head.

"Why does it matter?" I ask curiously.

He shakes his head roughly before releasing my arm. "I guess it doesn't."

Without him keeping me steady, I sway again, and like before; he grabs me again to keep me steady.

He gazes down at me in concern this time. "What's wrong with you, Piper?"

Thankfully, I don't have to answer because Cam wraps his arm around my waist and shoves Mason's hand from my arm.

"Nothing's wrong with her, so keep your hands off my girl." He growls before pulling me away towards the school.

"Why did you do that?" I ask curiously once we're alone in front of our locker that we were now going to be sharing.

"He was getting a bit too nosey. That and his scent is a little off. He might be someone dangerous." Cam answers me.

"Wouldn't you know if he was like us?" I question curiously.

He shakes his head. "No, the only way we know who's who is if we show our wings. Other than that, you can sometimes go by scent, but that doesn't always work. It does work, however, if there are wolves around."

My eyes widen, and he rolls his eyes as he shuts the locker and begins pulling me to our class. "I have a lot to teach you, Sis, and we'll begin when we get home later. But, for now, let's learn this silly human stuff."

I nod my head and allow him to lead me down the hall and to our first class.

****

Thankfully, all of our morning classes go by fast.

I'm beyond happy when lunchtime arrives.

Cam sits me down in a seat at an empty table before going to get our lunches. Sitting alone, I lay my head on the cool table, feeling way past exhausted.

"Can I sit here?"

Joel asks abruptly.

I look up to see his smiling face before I nod. "Yeah, you can, but it wouldn't be a very smart idea if your brother is around where he'll see us together."

He sits down next to me anyway.

I shake my head and bite my lip, holding back my grin.

"Are you feeling alright?" He asks while studying me closely.

"I'm just really tired," I answer truthfully.

He nods, accepting my response before he begins to eat the food on his lunch tray.

Without warning, Mason sits next to Joel, and we both tense and glance in each other's direction before we turn to watch him closely.

He begins eating silently, and I groan inwardly.

This was no doubt going to be painful.

Laying my head on the table again, I groan quietly while thumping it down against the hard surface a few times until Cam stops me.

"What's wrong, Sweetheart?" He questions, gaining my attention before he pushes my tray of food in front of me.

He rubs my back as he searches for an answer within my eyes.

"Nothing's wrong." I lie sarcastically, hoping that he would get my underlying message.

He nods once as his eyes shift to the others sitting at the table before turning back toward me.

"Nothing other than the awkward company, huh?" He snorts.

I nod while trying and failing to keep my grin hidden.

After a few moments of silence, I begin eating but stop again when Mason groans from his side of the table while Joel starts laughing into his hand.

"Can the girl never get the hint?" Mason growls quietly as an attractive young girl walks over to our table before sitting next to him.

She bats her lashes at him while placing her hand on his arm.

"Can I sit here, Mason?" She questions sweetly.

He shakes his head no, but she ignores him as she turns her attention to us.

"Who are your new friends?" She asks while pinning me with a glare.

I roll my eyes and sit back in my seat as I wait for the show to begin. This was normal for me, and I found myself almost eager to toy with her.

"I'm Piper, and this is Cam," I answer her.

She nods and smiles as her eyes rake over Cam before turning back to me.

"Why are you with her?" She questions him abruptly.

I grin menacingly, ready for this. She was going to play this game, but I was going to win.

"He's with me because I'm a good lay," I answer smugly.

She practically chokes on her breath, along with everyone else around the table.

Cam just chuckles beside me and pinches my side.

Her eyes quickly turn to Cam while he places his arm around my shoulders and his lips turn up in a cocky grin.

"She's right; no girl could ever compare to her moves." He laughs before kissing my cheek.

"You know your bad, right?" He whispers into my ear before leaning away.

I laugh out louder.

"You know you like my naughtiness," I answer loud enough for everyone to hear as I push him playfully.

He nods in agreement with a grin. "Yeah, I do."

"Well, if you ever get tired of her, I'm always free." The girl states with a cocky smile in my direction.

She really thought that she could outdo me, but she had another thing coming.

Cam just laughs and shakes his head. "I'll never get tired of her, but Mason over there looks in need of a good lay." Cam teases as he motions towards Mason.

We all laugh as Mason's eyes go wide.

Cam had just thrown him back under the bus in order to get the girl's attention away from us.

The girl giggles and then stands to whisper something into Mason's ear before walking off.

Once she's gone, Mason turns to Cam. "Why would you do that, man? Now she's never going to leave me alone. She's been at this for two years."

Cam shrugs and lays his hand on the back of my chair as he plays with the ends of my hair. "That was just payback for touching Piper earlier."

Mason nods.

Joel's jaw begins to tick again, and I absently reach for his hand under the table.

He had it balled into a fist, but I force it to open. His body instantly relaxes as my fingers slide in between his.

Seeing the gesture, Cam leans in toward me.

"What are you doing?" He asks quietly so no one else can hear.

"I'm keeping him calm. He was about to punch someone." I answer honestly.

His forehead creases in thought as he leans away from me for a moment. Leaning close again, Cam breathes in deeply.

He pulls back wide-eyed and curses while shaking his head roughly.

"Oh, crap." He then mutters.

"What's wrong, Cam?" I question, quickly becoming worried.

He only shakes his head in response, not wanting to talk here. I nod and then return to eating my lunch.

Joel releases my hand after a little while, and I breathe out, relieved.

Beth comes over to the table shyly and bows her head as she blushes and points to an empty chair at the table.

"Can I sit here?" She asks quietly.

"Of course you can, Beth," I answer brightly.

She sits down quietly with us before glancing around the table curiously. After a moment, her eyes land on me as she chuckles. "Boy, this table is tense."

I nod my agreement.

She then turns her attention to Mason with a raised eyebrow. "Why exactly are you here anyway? Last I heard, you hated Piper?"

"I do hate Piper." He answers with a huff.

"I will believe that when I see it, your eyes are telling me another story, mister." She replies.

Mason's eyes widen in shock while Cam chokes on his drink.

She then turns her attention to Cam.

He visibly gulps.

"And who exactly are you?" She asks while pointing a finger in his direction.

"I'm her boyfriend?" He answers, but it comes out more like a question.

I roll my eyes and pinch his side.

"This is Cam, and yes, he's my boyfriend. He just doesn't realize the trouble he's in for yet," I answer Beth.

She nods her head before she begins eating her food.

"You're a ton of trouble, aren't you?" Cam laughs as he leans in close again.

"You have no idea," I reply.

Without warning, Joel suddenly slams his fist down on the table with a hard crack, effectively making us all jump.

He stands to his feet and looks down at me with unbridled anger.

"When exactly did he become your boyfriend, Piper? Was it before or after we kissed only a few days ago? I'm wondering because you have confused the hell out of me. One day you're jumping me, and the next, you show up with him, and then not just ten minutes ago, you were holding my hand under the table." He growls.

I swear every eye in the room focuses on me.

I turn to Beth for help, but she just continues munching away on her food like she was watching a daytime TV show.

She wasn't going to be any help at all. So, I would have to deal with this all on my own.

I stand to my feet while begging him with my eyes to just calm down, but instead of calming down, he only seems to grow angrier.

There was only one option left for me at this point to calm him down and get him to understand what was going on.

I had to tell him the truth.

Grabbing his arm, I pull him away from the table and then out into the empty hall.

I lean against the wall while still holding his hand. "Joel, I hate this, I really do. I want to be completely honest with you, but you have to promise not to tell anyone what I'm about to tell you, okay?"

He nods and moves closer.

I let out a soft sigh when his hand brushes my cheek. "Tell me what's going on. This is killing me to see you with him."

Nodding, I take a deep breath before releasing it slowly.

"I'm sick, Joel. Cam is here because of that, and he's helping me hide it. He's not really my boyfriend; he's my half-brother." I explain while bowing my head.

His fingers lift my chin to look into his eyes.

"Why are you sick?" He asks.

I shake my head. I couldn't tell him the truth, at least not the whole truth.

"I've been getting really weak. I don't exactly know what's going on, but I found out it runs in the family. That's why Cam is here. He's dealt with this before." I answer.

He nods, thankfully believing my words.

"You know you could have asked me for help, Piper. I don't care what Mason says. I still want to be around you. I want a chance to be with you." He confesses.

I smile. "I'd like that too, Joel, but for now, we need to play this off so no one finds out how sick I actually am, okay?"

"Fine, but I'll only agree if you kiss me right now." He replies with a smirk.

I grin as he leans in and presses his lips against mine.

His hands rest on my hips while my tongue dances with his. I quickly find myself completely intoxicated with him.

I couldn't get enough.

"I can't get enough of you, Piper." Joel groans softly as he pulls away, only to smash his lips back to mine once again.

"What the…?" Cam trails off with a low snarl as he walks into the hall.

Joel pulls back and smiles down at me.

"I told him, Cam. He knows that you're my brother." I confess quickly while leaning my forehead against Joel's chest.

"Like hell, I don't care what you told him." He growls and then points to Joel. "Whatever she told you is a lie, she likes to play games, and this will only end badly for you. She always comes back to me."

Joel takes a step back, believing Cam's lie.

I shake my head, angry with Cam, as I turn my full attention toward him.

"I hate you, Cam. I absolutely hate you for this." I growl out.

He grins wickedly before leaving Joel and me alone again.

Cam had ruined every bit of progress that I had just made with Joel, and I knew Joel wasn't going to believe anything I had to say.

Instead of trying to convince him that Cam had been lying, I keep my head bowed, waiting for his hate-filled words.

"I can't believe you lied to me, Piper," Joel whispers.

I close my eyes as I fight the tears that were threatening to fall. I stay silent, knowing my words wouldn't mean anything.

"This…whatever we had is over. I can't believe I honestly thought that just maybe I could have a real relationship with you." He mutters and then throws his hands into the air when I remain silent.

My heart was breaking, though.

Joel had been the first guy I had actually had growing feelings for, and I had really thought that I could have had a genuine relationship with him too.

"You must be a real tramp if you're always cheating on him, you know." He pauses a moment before continuing. "I don't even want to look at you anymore." He growls furiously before finally walking off.

Once he disappears, I slide down the wall, finally allowing the damn holding back my tears to break. They begin to pour down my cheeks, and I wipe them away frantically.

Of course, that's the exact moment when the pain starts again.

I sob harder and bite my lip to hold in my cries of pain.

For a few moments, I pray for death. I welcome it. I didn't want this life anymore. I didn't want to feel as lonely as I did right then for another day.

I just wanted to be an ordinary teenage girl in love. Was that too much to ask for?

When I'm about to lose control, Beth runs out and kneels next to me.

She takes my face into her hands.

"What's wrong, Piper?" She asks with growing concern as she searches my eyes.

"Get Cam, please. Tell him the pain is back. He'll know what to do." I barely pant out just before my world goes black as I pass out.

Chapter Five

"**H**ow many more times is she going to have to go through this, Michael?" Mom asks from somewhere in the distance.

"Well, how long will it be until her eighteenth birthday?" He asks.

I groan. I still had four more days.

I tune them out as I roll onto my stomach, burying my face into my pillow while wondering for a few moments how I had gotten here.

100

To be honest, I didn't care.

I felt horrible, and I could still taste blood in my mouth.

The door to my room opens and then closes quietly before Cam walks into my line of sight as I turn my head to the side.

I turn my head away from him, not wanting to talk.

He sighs sadly before the bed dips with his weight as he sits beside me.

"I know you're mad at me, Piper, but what I did was for your own good and his. I have so much that I need to teach you about being a dark Nephilim. I will tell you why I was so mean, and hopefully, you'll forgive me." He pauses for a few minutes.

I finally turn my head back to him, wanting to know his reasons.

He smiles and then continues. "You see, we all have certain scents, as I told you earlier, but with dark angels and Nephilim, we have a unique scent that attracts others to us. It acts as a drug, and the feeling they think they are feeling isn't really real. Do you understand so far?"

I nod. "I think so. So, do you really think that I put Joel under this kind of spell-like trance or whatever?"

He nods in response.

"So, he probably has no feelings whatsoever for me?" I whisper sadly.

Cam nods again.

Tears once again build in my eyes.

"I'm sorry, Sis." He apologizes. "This life isn't the easiest. We're not made for good purposes. We're nothing but tricksters. We feed off of negative energy."

Wiping my tears away, I sigh. "Okay, so let me see if I get this, we feed off of others' pain and suffering, and we're made to trick and deceive?"

"That pretty much sums it up; like I said before, you still have a lot to learn. Being a dark Nephilim is not easy, especially when you want to be good like our dad and me. We fight daily to keep ourselves hidden from other dark angels because if they discover that we are not doing the job we were made for, they will torture us." He explains.

"Wait, what?" I ask, stunned. "They'll really torture us if we don't deceive and torment others?"

He nods, and I curse.

"How did I get away from doing it for so long?" I ask tensely.

He shakes his head. "The only thing I can think of is that they never expected a female to be a dark Nephilim. Light and dark Nephilim are always males. So, you're the first-ever female."

"What does that mean for me in the long term?" I inquire next.

Cam sighs roughly before answering me. "It means that if others find out, some will be mad and want to harm you or even destroy you, but others will want you for the simple reason of using you to create pure dark angels."

I let out a huff of air. "Wow, this is just so much to take in, Cam."

"Yeah, I can imagine, but Dad and I are here for you no matter what happens." He promises.

After a moment, he stands to leave the room.

Reaching my hand out to grab onto his arm, I stop him.

"Hey, Cam, how long did you go through this change?" I ask, changing the subject.

He bows his head as he turns around to face me.

"I only went through it once. Most others only go through it twice, at the most." He answers truthfully.

"Do you think it's going to happen more for me?" I ask even though I already knew the answer to my question.

"I really want to tell you that it won't, but that would be a lie. You still have four more days until your birthday, and I'm almost certain those days will be pure hell for you." He pauses and then sits down next to me again before running his hands along my wings. "Honestly, you might not make it through this."

"I will make it, Cam. I know I will, but not without you or… Dad's help." I whisper out the last part considering it still felt weird to call Michael; Dad.

"We will always be here for you now, Piper." Michael chimes in as he walks into the room before sitting next to Cam. "We're family, and we'll fight this together. We will keep each other safe."

"Well, I better go. I have work I need to get done before the night is over." Cam sighs and then stands to his feet, giving me a quick wink before leaving.

Dad and I watch as he disappears down the hallway.

I sigh and turn my attention toward Dad. "He's off to create mayhem, isn't he?"

Dad nods sadly. "Yes, he is. I'm glad he talked to you about that. We'll have to take drastic steps to keep you hidden now, especially once you turn eighteen. I'm going to need you to start working with Cam. That's the only way we're going to be able to keep you hidden."

I nod. "I'll do whatever you need me to do, Michael…um, I mean, Dad."

"You don't have to call me Dad, Piper. I know this is still hard for you to grasp." He replies.

"Thanks, but I really should call you Dad since that's what you are. Plus, I think I kind of like saying it." I laugh, and he smiles broadly.

"Are your wings feeling any better?" He asks, changing the subject.

I groan softly as I flap them.

"I guess so, but I'm almost too exhausted to move them," I answer honestly.

"Well, here, take some more of my blood. It should help you heal better and give you a little more energy." He insists while holding out his wrist that he had already cut open for me.

Pushing up on my arms, I try to position myself on my side so I can sit up, but my arms give out, and I fall back onto the bed.

Without a word, Michael helps me to sit up slightly so that I was in the proper position to bring his wrist to my mouth.

I start sucking the blood into my mouth, and as he runs his fingers through my hair in a soothing fatherly way, I close my eyes as tears slip from them.

I didn't know why I was crying; I just felt the need to.

"I'm scared, Daddy," I admit in a whisper as I continue to cry while pulling away from him once I'm done drinking down his blood.

"I know you are, Sweetheart. I'm here for you, though." He assures me.

Nodding, I relax face down on the bed once more until the horrible pain washes over me again.

I begin sobbing, begging for it to stop, but it doesn't.

It rakes over my battered body over and over, relentlessly. I scream out, pleading for it just to go away.

There's a moment when I even beg for death.

And just when I think I can't take anymore, a bright light flashes in the room, and a sudden wave of relief washes over me.

I take a deep breath and turn my head to where the bright light still shines.

My father and another angel were standing face to face.

Fear is written all over my father's face, which in turn scares me.

"You cannot tell anyone, please, Gabriel." Michael pleads.

"I won't say a word to anyone. I'm only here to help." Gabriel answers as his wings fold away, causing the bright light to disappear.

"What brought you here, Gabriel?" Dad then asks curiously as he watches Gabriel move to sit next to me on my bed.

"I could hear her screams." He whispers. "I could almost feel her pain. It nearly crippled my sons."

"Are we in danger of others coming?" Dad questions, becoming alarmed.

Thankfully, Gabriel shakes his head. "No, there is no danger; I just live nearby."

His hand then brushes my hair away from my face as he smiles down at me.

"You are just as pretty as my son told me." He whispers before a wave of pure pleasure washes over me, canceling out the pain.

A moment later, I fade into a deep sleep.

As I slipped into the darkness, I could only wonder who he had been talking about. Who did I know that would have spoken about me that way?

Who would have taken notice of me other than Joel and Mason? Both of them more than likely hated me now, so they were out of the question.

So, who else could it be?

****

Hours later, I wake up to find Cam sitting with me, my head resting in his lap as he runs his hands absently over my wings.

I smile up at him, and he grins.

"Feeling better?" He asks quietly.

I nod. "Yeah, a little. How bad was it this time?"

He stays quiet for a few moments before answering. "It was really bad, Piper, really, really, bad. I couldn't even fix your wings fast enough on my own. So, dad and Gabriel had to help me."

"How long have I been asleep this time?" I question next.

He looks around the room absently before sighing. "About six hours. It's early morning now."

"Is that Gabriel guy, or whatever, still here?" I then inquire, hopeful.

He nods, and I continue. "Can you take me to him?"

He nods again. "I can; he's in the kitchen with Dad and your mom."

Moving carefully, he slides out from under me and then stands to his feet as I will my wings to fold up. I'm thankful when they do without any pain or trouble.

Cam smiles widely while holding out his hand to me. I stand to my feet, and his arm immediately snakes around my waist to hold me upright.

As we make our way downstairs, I think of something that I should have asked days ago.

"How old are you, Cam?" I blurt.

He bellows out a laugh as we come to a stop at the bottom of the stairs.

"Are you sure you want to know?" He questions while grinning. I nod, and he continues. "Alright, but remember, I warned you." He pauses dramatically for a moment. "I'm one hundred and ten years old. I'll be one-hundred and eleven, right on your birthday."

"Holy… how's that even possible?" I stutter out in utter disbelief.

"Once we hit age eighteen, our bodies almost stop aging. Nothing can kill us other than pure angels, so our life spans are long." He explains as we begin walking again.

"Dad is over five thousand years old if you can believe that." He adds.

"Wow. So, wait, you share my birthday?" I ask.

He nods. "I sure do."

As we finally make our way into the kitchen, where my mom, sister, Dad, and Gabriel are all sitting at the table, Cam clears his throat to gain their attention.

They all look up at us and smile.

"It's good to see you up, Sweetheart." Mom states happily.

"Thanks, Mom, but I'm only up because I wanted to thank Gabriel," I answer.

She nods with a smile.

"No need to thank me, Piper." Gabriel insists as he stands up while Cam and I make our way over to him.

As we step up in front of him, he wraps his arm around my waist, replacing Cam's hold on me before helping me into his vacated seat.

"I still feel I have to, though. You helped to take the pain away. So, thank you for that." I argue lightly.

"You welcome." He replies with a smile while sitting in another chair next to me.

"How are you feeling, Piper?" Hannah chimes in quietly.

"I'm fine, Hannah. You know you don't need to worry about me. I'm just a little weak, but I'll be fine soon." I lie easily.

She nods.

"Hannah, why don't you and I head to bed so these guys can talk?" Mom insists with a yawn as she stands to her feet.

Hannah nods again with a yawn of her own.

I watch silently as they walk away before disappearing from view. I felt so far away from them at this moment, even though they were only feet away.

Sighing softly, I turn to look at Cam. "I'm going to have to watch them die, aren't I?"

He glances in the direction that they had left and then back to me with a single nod.

"It's one of the worst things about this life. We always have to watch the humans around us grow old and die." Cam whispers sadly.

Clearly, he must have had to watch someone close to him die.

"I agree, it isn't an easy life, and it will be much harder for you. I still can't wrap my head around this. I can't believe an actual dark female Nephilim was born. We must keep you hidden at all costs." Gabriel states while Dad and Cam both nod along.

"What are you exactly? I know you're not exactly like us, which means you're a light angel?" I ask curiously.

"Yes, I am. I'm a pure light angel." He answers proudly.

"And you said before that you have sons. Do I know them?" I inquire next.

"Yes, I have two sons." He answers but then glances toward my father, who shakes his head no slightly. "I don't believe you know them, though."

That was a lie.

I arch an eyebrow. "I know you're lying, but I'm not going to start a fight to get answers. You must have your reasons to lie."

Gabriel snorts in amusement before shaking his head. "I'm sorry. I just don't want them involved in this just yet. It's for all of our safeties."

He then turns to my father with a grin. "She's definitely yours, Michael. She can spot a liar from a mile away."

"Of course, she can. It's our job to be on top of things like that, especially if we can use it to our advantage," Dad answers proudly.

"I know that all too well, Michael. One question I have, though, is how you're going to get her virginity past the others. They're going to be able to smell it a mile away, and if she's anywhere near either of you two, it will look suspicious." Gabriel states next.

My eyes widen as I look at my father, who bows his head.

"I know it's a problem, and I haven't yet talked to her, but we're going to have to do something about it." Dad answers.

I gasp as anger washes over me.

Cam curses, and I stand to my feet.

"That's one thing I will not just give up. I want one thing in my life to be under my control, and that's honestly the only thing that I have been able to control. I'm waiting for the right person, and I won't go against that belief. So, if you think for one minute…." I trail off as Cam grabs me around my waist.

"Shhhh, Sis, we never said you had to. We just have to find a way to keep that part hidden." He assures me.

He continues to hold me tightly as the fight flees from my body before my body grows exhausted once again. My knees buckle, but he manages to keep me upright until my wings decide to come out on their own, pushing him away from me.

I fall forward and cry out as pain once again takes its punishment out on me.

"Dad, this shouldn't be happening so often. She hasn't even had a chance to rest." Cam cries out as he once again grabs hold of me.

I bury my face against his chest and sob.

They all stay silent around me, but when the pain fades a fraction, I look up at them.

Their eyes are wide as they look past me to my wings. I close my eyes and whimper, not wanting to even know.

Biting my lip, I barely hold back my cries as I bury my head back into Cam's chest.

"I have never seen that happen." Cam whispers.

I cringe. It wasn't good if he hadn't seen it before.

"I've heard of it, but I haven't seen it either. How about you, Gabriel?" Dad asks.

"I've only seen it once, and it changes everything. We have to keep her hidden. In the wrong hands, she could destroy us all." Gabriel answers, sounding a bit panicked.

"What does it mean, Gabriel?" Dad pleads.

"It means that she can kill purebred angels. She also has the unique ability to change us from light to dark or dark to light," Gabriel replies.

"How can she possibly kill us…?" Dad's voice trails off as I let out another scream while sharp pain slices through my jaw, making it feel as if someone was tearing it in two.

Pushing Cam away, I cry out, terrified, as blood begins pouring out of my mouth and down my throat.

"That's how she can kill us, Michael," Gabriel answers while pointing in my direction.

Cam and Michael gasp before letting out strings of curses.

The pain fades completely away before I run my tongue across four very sharp fangs descending from either side of my two front teeth.

Tears begin pouring from my eyes as I look at my father in fear.

"What are we going to do now, Gabriel?" Dad asks softly.

"We have no choice but to keep what she is a secret. Unfortunately, it's going to be hard now because she not only has to feed off of chaos and mayhem, she will also need to feed on angel blood." He explains.

"So, essentially, you're telling us that Piper is a vampire slash angel?" Cam questions curiously.

Gabriel nods. "Yes, and she can kill us by drinking our blood, but if she learns restraint, she can feed without doing any harm."

"I don't want any of this. I don't want to hurt anyone." I cry out as Cam tries to wrap his arms around me once more.

I try but fail to push him away, and as I bury my face into the crook of his neck, an overwhelming hunger takes hold.

"Piper, stop," Michael commands.

I ignore him and wrap my arms around Cam tightly.

He lets out a string of curses, realizing the danger he had put himself into.

"Wait, she needs this, right?" Cam presses and then stays silent for a moment before he continues. "She needs to learn how to control herself, so who better than us to teach her."

"Are you sure you want to put yourself into this sort of danger, Son?" Michael asks.

Cam nods without hesitating.

"Go ahead, Piper. I know you won't hurt me." He then whispers down to me.

I smile against his skin. I had been ready to bite him either way, but to have his permission fills me with a deeper hunger.

With my fangs scrapping against his skin, I sigh softly, stopping myself. I pull back for a moment to look into his trusting eyes.

"I won't hurt you, Cam," I promise.

His eyes soften, and his pupils dilate as he nods absently.

Frowning, I look over to Gabriel, who seemed to have all the answers.

"Your scent, it's causing him to relax so you can feed freely. It's acting as a powerful sedative." He answers my unspoken question.

My lips form an 'o' as I nod.

"Please, stop me if I hurt him," I stress.

Both Michael and Gabriel nod in agreement.

Glancing back at Cam's face, I move my lips back to his neck. My new fangs throb with an ache before I open my mouth slightly, almost too afraid to bite him.

I didn't want to harm anyone, especially not my brother.

Closing my eyes tightly, I bite into his skin. His blood fills my mouth, and I cringe before it hits my tongue.

I half expected the taste to be horrid. Instead, it tastes much like chocolate.

Groaning, I lap it up quickly, not wanting to waste a drop. When I realize what I'm doing, I quickly pull away, hoping that I hadn't caused any damage.

Both Gabriel and Michael look at me proudly as I hold onto Cam. I lick his neck once, and the four puncture holes from my fangs heal before my eyes.

I grin, pleased with myself, as I look up at Cam's smiling face.

He looked the same as before, and I let out a breath of relief.

"You did very well, Piper, better than I thought you would. This may not be so hard for you to control after all." Gabriel states.

"That was by far the hardest thing I've ever done, Gabriel. The only reason I stopped was because it was Cam. What happens if I feed on someone I don't care for?" I bite out before I release Cam and stalk over to my father.

"You will be able to control this, Piper. I know you will," Michael answers with conviction.

I wasn't so sure, though.

Chapter Six

Sitting in my room later, I try time after time to put away my new dark red wings. I didn't want to see them any longer.

And I definitely didn't like what they represented.

"Why won't you just go away?" I huff out before lying face down on my bed, screaming my frustration into my pillow to keep the sound muffled.

"Are you alright in here, Sis?" Cam questions suddenly before walking in and then sitting on the edge of my bed.

I turn my head just enough to glare at him, and he grins wickedly. "Go away, Cam."

He shakes his head. "Nope, I'm not going anywhere. I want you to come with me tonight. Your pain hasn't returned, so I think it's safe for us to go out and work."

"How can I go anywhere when my wings won't disappear?" I question sarcastically.

"First of all, you can't be angry at them. If you would only calm down and relax, then you'd find that they'll go away a lot easier." He explains simply.

"How am I supposed to calm down after everything that I just found out, Cam?" I ask before burying my face back into my pillow.

"I don't know, but you can't stay in your room and mope around forever. You need to go out and have a little bit of fun." He answers.

His hands begin rubbing soothing circles down my back, and I finally start to relax. True to his words, my wings easily disappear on their own after a few moments.

I roll to my side as Cam sits there with a smug grin playing on his lips.

His mouth opens to speak, but I hold my finger to his lips to stop him.

"Don't even say it. I won't listen. You were right. That's all you're ever going to get out of me." I take my finger away and sigh. "What kind of fun did you have in mind exactly?"

He smiles brightly. "We're going to go dancing."

"Dancing...?" I ask with a raised brow as he stands to his feet.

"Yes, so wear something sexy. I'll be right back so we can take off." He replies before walking out my door without another word.

I huff out a breath and place my head back on my pillow.

Closing my eyes, I think of what I could wear.

****

Twenty minutes later, Cam rushes back into my room, looking rather dashing in a pair of dark-wash jeans and a tight black shirt.

I laugh a little and twirl around to show him my outfit: a black low-cut halter top with a matching mini skirt.

He lets out a low whistle while sitting down on my bed.

"Are you ready to go break some hearts?" He asks with a grin.

I nod before sitting down next to him to slip on my knee-high black boots.

This elicits another low whistle, and I shove him playfully.

"I'm ready whenever you are." I laugh before standing back on my feet.

He stands, too, before holding his arm out for me to slip my arm through.

Making our way downstairs, we pass our father going up.

He stops for a moment to look at us both and smiles. "Be careful tonight, don't do anything too crazy, and if you need me for anything, just call."

"We will be, Dad. No need to worry. We'll be back before you know it." Cam replies as he begins tugging me the rest of the way down the stairs and then out the front door.

"Hey, Cam, how exactly are we getting to wherever we're going?" I inquire curiously as we walk over to the garage.

He grins mischievously, and I roll my eyes, realizing what our only source of transportation would be.

I should have worn pants for this.

"How else would we get there, other than in style? By the way, you should have worn jeans, but it will drive the guys crazy to see your legs when we pull up." He replies with a mischievous smirk playing on his lips.

I roll my eyes again as he disappears into the garage and then returns moments later, pushing my bike out.

I smile as he hops on the back and then holds it steady for me.

Hiking up my skirt, I throw my leg over it as he laughs.

I pinch his side while he starts the engine before we take off down the driveway and then out onto the road.

As we ride down the road, I force myself not to look at Joel and Mason's house, but I fail.

I glance over and sigh, I didn't know what I was expecting, but it hurt to see Joel walking to a car with another girl.

It made me want to scream, but I hold it all in.

There hadn't been any truth to our relationship anyway, just crazy pheromones.

I lay my head against Cam's back as Joel looks our way. His frown is clearly visible until Mason steps out of his house with another woman and a man who looks a lot like Mason.

I continue to watch as the others get into the car while Mason stops next to Joel and frowns.

After a few more seconds, I close my eyes, not wanting to see their reactions any longer.

****

Fifteen short minutes later, we drive past a long line of people that were waiting to get into a large brick building.

Everyone's eyes turn to us as Cam slows down and then pulls into a parking space near the front.

He turns off the bike and then glances back at me with a grin.

"You ready for this, Piper? Can you feel their jealousy?" He questions quietly.

I take a deep breath and nod my head as my senses are filled with a new kind of energy that I had never felt before.

"It's amazing, isn't it?" He asks.

I nod again. It was a powerful feeling, intoxicating even.

"Yeah, it's amazing. Does it feel like this every time you go out?" I ask while sliding off the bike gracefully.

"It gets much better." He promises as he gets off the bike next.

I raise my brow in question, wondering how it could get better, as he holds out his arm. After I thread my arm through his, he pulls me to the front of the line and up to a rather large bouncer.

The man lowers his dark glasses and grins at us before bumping his knuckles with Cam.

"You finally brought a date with you tonight, huh, Cameron?" He asks.

Cam's grin widens as he glances toward me for a brief second. "Of course. I told you that I would someday, didn't I?"

They laugh before the man holds his hand out for me to shake.

"Piper, meet Duke, Duke, meet my girl, Piper." Cam introduces us.

Duke holds my hand for a moment, and I playfully bat my lashes at him. He grins wider as he lets my hand go before opening the door for us.

The people still waiting in the line begin to yell out in anger and frustration, but we ignore them as we walk in.

As I pass, I trail my hand over Duke's arm, and his grin turns dark.

Cam grabs me around the waist before pointing his finger at Duke in mock anger. "Stay away from her, Duke; she's mine."

Duke shakes his head in response while waving us on.

"I'm yours, huh?" I tease once we step inside.

He rolls his eyes. "For tonight, you are. You jump when I say jump, okay." He orders lightly. "I don't want you to get hurt, but I do want you to have fun."

I laugh and give him a two-finger salute. "Yes, Sir, when you say jump, I'll jump."

He shakes his head in amusement as we make our way down the dark hallway and into a large room booming with music.

Everyone's energy seeps deep into my bones and grin.

It was utterly intoxicating.

"I'm going to go dance, Cam," I yell over the music as I point toward the area where a mass of bodies are already dancing.

He nods. "I'll be over at the bar if you need me. Please stay where I can see you, though."

I nod before moving over to the crowded dance floor.

As I close my eyes and dance to the fast pace of the music, I finally find peace; my mind relaxes as I sway with the bodies that begin to pack in closely around me.

Every so often, I glance at the bar where Cam is watching me. He gives me a salute with his drink before turning back to the bar.

Girls surround him from every angle, and I smile, I knew the insane amount of jealousy we were going to cause tonight, and I found that it excited me.

It was going to be epic.

I close my eyes once more as strong hands grab onto my hips. I sway with the person, not even caring who it could be, just enjoying the moment.

My mind jumps to wanting those hands to be Joel's, but I quickly shake that thought away. He hated me now, but it was probably for the best.

Suddenly, another set of hands grab me from the front, and I open my eyes, thinking that they are Cam's, but my eyes go wide with shock when I see Mason standing in front of me.

He smiles down at me while pulling my body close to his.

I could easily feel every contour of his body, every tense muscle through his thin shirt.

His head dips to my neck before he trails his lips along my skin to my ear. "What are you doing here, Piper?"

I lick my lips and shake my head slightly.

"Who was leaving your house earlier?" I question, changing the subject away from myself.

"It was my mom, my sister, and my other brother. They're leaving town for a bit." He answers quickly before pinning me with a look. "Now, answer my question, Piper. Why are you here?"

"I can do what I want, Mason, but if you must know, I came here with Cam. We're on a date." I answer.

He pulls back to look around at the crowd before leaning in close again. "I don't see him here."

I frown and look over to the bar where he should have been. I then glance around and curse when I don't see him anywhere.

The hands behind me suddenly disappear, and I sigh in relief as Cam's familiar hands grab onto me, pulling me back against his body.

"Back off, man, she's mine." He growls in warning.

Mason doesn't back off, though; he only grins with challenge before pulling me forward, back against his body.

"Let me have this dance with her, and then you can have her back. I need to talk to her for a minute." Mason replies.

I glance back to Cam and nod that I'd be okay.

He watches me for a moment before cursing and then walking away.

"Say what you need to say, Mason," I yell loud enough to be heard over the music as I focus on his face.

He places his hands firmly on my hips and spins me around so my back is to his front. His hands then trail down my thighs, and I throw my head back as we dance together.

Again, his head dips to place his lips near my ear.

"You really hurt my brother, you know." He breathes out.

I nod in response, not wanting to talk about it. He then grinds up against me, and I lace my arms back around his neck.

"Is Cam really your boyfriend?" He inquires next.

I turn in his arms and look into his eyes. I needed to lie to him, but I find myself shaking my head ever so slightly.

His eyes narrow before I lean in to whisper in his ear.

"He's my brother. He's only trying to protect me. I didn't want to hurt Joel, but we weren't good together. I would have hurt him, in the end, no matter what." I answer honestly.

"You finally saw why I didn't want you two together, then?" He asks.

I nod and close my eyes for a brief moment.

"I have to confess that I didn't want you two together for other reasons, as well." He admits abruptly while grinning bashfully.

I raise my brow in question. "What other reason would you have?"

He dips his head close once again to my ear to answer. He remains quiet for a moment as his lips feather against my skin.

"I wanted you for myself. From the moment I saw you standing outside in your front yard, I have wanted you all to myself." He confesses before pulling away and then leaving me altogether.

I stand in the middle of the swaying crowd, frozen in shock. Had Mason really just confessed to me that he wanted me?

Cam moves up to me quickly while looking around. His arms wrap around me before he pulls me off the dance floor and then over to the bar.

I sit on a stool absently, and Cam orders me a drink as he stands beside me.

"What did he want, Piper?" He then demands.

"I think he just admitted to having feelings for me," I whisper, still in shock.

"He does?" He asks in surprise while looking back into the crowd absently.

"Yes, I think he does." I sigh and then swiftly swallow the shot glass the bartender places in front of me.

The liquid burns my throat as it goes down.

"I think I want him, too," I add, causing Cam to groan.

Shaking his head, my attention falls on him. "You can't have a relationship, Piper, at least not with a human. It's just not going to work. Your pheromones are what's making him attracted to you anyway. That's not a relationship."

"I just want a normal life, Cam. That's all I ever wanted," I confess sadly while bowing my head.

He takes my chin in his hand, lifting it to look into his eyes. "I know that, Sis, but we can't change what we are. I know you'll find someone, but for now, you have to be careful."

I nod my head and turn back to look at the dancing crowd while plastering on a smile.

"I'm going to go dance some more," I state, taking another drink and then one more that the bartender brings for Cam.

They both chuckle before I stand and then make my way back over to the dance floor.

Again, strong hands grab my hips from behind, and I lean back into the person's embrace.

His lips trail up my neck as I throw my hands behind his head. His hands then slowly glide over the exposed skin of my stomach, and I moan inwardly.

"You are an exquisite dancer, Sweetheart." The man's voice whispers into my ear, causing me to shiver.

"Your smell is quite intoxicating as well. It makes me wonder if our dear Michael knows what his daughter truly is." He adds.

I turn in his arms, suddenly alarmed.

"Who are you?" I whisper while searching his dark eyes.

He smiles down at me as his hands grab onto my hips, pulling me closer to him again.

"I am Marcus, and you do not need to fear me." He answers softly.

"How do you know what I am?" I question next, causing his grin to widen.

"I've been watching you." He replies easily.

"Why haven't you shown your face until now?" I push, confused.

"I haven't had others in my way to get what I wanted until now." He answers while pulling my body flush with his.

His hand presses against my back, and I sigh softly, feeling comfortable in his embrace.

"What are you doing here, Marcus?" Cam clips out as he pulls me away seconds later before shoving me behind him.

"I'm only doing my job, Cam, the same as you two. No harm done." He replies, holding his hands up in surrender.

Cam curses while looking around at the crowd watching us closely.

"We have to make this look good, and if I'm going to have to deal with you, then I want to be drunk with power." Cam finally answers.

Marcus grins.

I'm stuck looking at both of them as they turn their attention toward me.

"Can someone fill me in on this real quick?" I ask before Cam pulls me in between the two of them, turning me to face him.

His head dips down, and he sighs in my ear. "Marcus is good, but I don't get along with him most of the time. He's here now to help us work. We obviously weren't doing a good enough job. Just go along with whatever we do so we don't end up on the wrong radar, okay."

He pulls away, and I nod in understanding.

Marcus turns me to face him, and his head comes down next so he can speak to me, or at least that's what I thought until his lips softly caress my skin.

Suddenly, the hunger I had felt earlier in the day comes rushing back, making my veins feel as if they were crawling under my skin.

I gasp out as my fangs suddenly descend.

Marcus pulls back, and his eyes go wide before he looks over my shoulder to Cam in question.

"You're hungry again?" Cam asks from behind, and I nod. "Tell Marcus what you need. He can help."

I nod once more as I glance up at Marcus's confused face.

Fear overrides my actions, though, and instead of talking to Marcus, I pull away from their grasp and then take off running toward the bathrooms.

I didn't want to hurt anyone.

Both Cam and Marcus yell out to me as they follow behind me. I ignore them as I push and shove my way through the crowd.

The hunger grows fiercely inside me as I continue to force people out of my way roughly, not caring that some of them fall to the floor.

When I suddenly slam into a rigid body, I look up into Mason's worried gaze and practically scream out with joy.

He grabs my hand roughly before dragging me into a secluded corner.

"What's wrong?" He inquires.

I bow my head, trying to hide my face from him. I didn't want him to see my fangs.

His hand gently lifts my chin, and when he sees a few of my tears streaming down my cheeks, he wipes them away. "Please, tell me what's wrong, Babe."

"I can't," I whisper.

He shakes his head roughly.

"Yes, you can. There's nothing that you can tell me that will make me leave you like this." He pushes.

I look deep into his eyes for a moment, and just as I'm just about to reveal my secret to him, Marcus grabs me from behind and turns me to face him before his lips press against mine.

Cam grabs me from his arms suddenly and then thankfully drags me away.

"We need to go now, Piper." He growls while pulling me through the club.

I glance back to see Marcus and Mason in a heated discussion.

For a moment, I wonder what they could possibly be fighting about, or how they even knew each other considering Marcus was like us and…well…Mason wasn't.

Cam pulls me through a side door and then out into a deserted alley.

I take a deep breath of fresh air but groan when the hunger again rears its ugly head.

Turning towards Cam, I begin stalking him with vicious intent.

He throws his hands up as I back him against the nearest wall. "Hold on just a few more seconds, Piper. You can't feed from me again so soon. Marcus will be out to help; just hold on."

"I'm so hungry, though, Cam, it hurts." I cry out, pained.

He nods in understanding. "Just hold on as long as you can."

I look back as the same door we had come through opens, and Marcus walks through. He, too, throws his hands up in surrender as I turn to him with a fierce growl.

"Easy now, Piper. Calm down for a second, and I'll feed you." He commands.

I nod even though I don't stop moving toward him.

As I stop with my face just mere inches from his, he stands up straighter and then takes a step forward toward me.

It was a show of dominance, and I couldn't help but back down. I take a step back and then another as he continues to move forward.

My back soon hits the same wall that I had had Cam pinned up at.

Pressing his body against mine, Marcus's hand comes up to caress my cheek. I lean into it absently and close my eyes for a brief moment.

"Cam, can you stop her when I say?" He asks softly while still looking deep into my eyes.

"Yes, I can. Just tell me when," Cam answers from beside us.

Marcus's hands grab onto my hips, sliding down to my thighs before he lifts me to hold my body up and against the wall as he moves his head so that I can access his neck.

I grin and lick my lips before quickly biting into him, moaning softly as his blood fills my mouth.

He pushes forward into me with a low moan of his own, and I grin against his skin, enjoying his reaction.

Everything around us fades away. All my mind could focus on was his heartbeat and the sweet taste of his blood filling my mouth.

I barely notice when the doorway to the building opens.

But when a familiar face comes into view, I pause.

"Seriously, Cam, you're just going to stand there and watch while your girlfriend gets screwed by another guy?" Joel bites out.

I stop drinking Marcus's blood and lick the wound closed.

As I pull back, Marcus looks at me in question before I bow my head in shame, realizing what this must look like to anyone else.

"I'm glad I dodged that crazy train; you both make me sick." Joel spits out in disgust before he leaves.

Tears begin pouring down my cheeks as Marcus places me back down to my feet.

I move away from him as Cam moves over to me.

"Don't listen to him, Sis. He has no idea what's going on, and even if he did, he would never understand." Cam whispers while reaching up to dry my tears.

"I just want to go home, Cam, now, please," I beg.

He nods before looking at Marcus.

"Can you take her home for me?" He questions him. "I still need to work."

"I can; I've finished for the night," Marcus answers with a nod. "I need to talk with Michael anyway. We have some things we need to discuss since I revealed myself. I'm going to need his protection."

Cam gives me a quick hug before walking back into the building.

I hug my arms to myself, feeling uncomfortable, until Marcus wraps his arms around me with a sad sigh. "Don't let his words bother you, Sweetheart. You're more than that, and you know it."

I study his dark brown eyes as he steps back.

His hand runs through his short shaggy brown hair as he begins to smile.

"Thank you, Marcus," I whisper.

He shakes his head. "Don't thank me, Sweetheart. I only speak the truth."

He then holds his arm out for me, and I wrap my arm around his waist as we walk down the alley and then toward his car together.

Leaning my head against his side, I close my eyes, allowing him to guide me.

Once we're in his car, I remain quiet until we pull up to my house.

As Marcus turns the engine off and is about to get out, I grab his arm, stopping him.

"Why have you been following me?" I ask curiously.

It had been bothering me since he had admitted to it when we had been back in the club together.

He bows his head and looks up at me through his dark lashes. "I was protecting you, keeping you safe, just in case...." He trails off.

"You knew this was going to happen to me, didn't you?" I blurt in disbelief.

He nods. "I had a feeling that it would."

I turn to look straight out the front windshield, not knowing what to say.

He sighs sadly, and I glance over at him.

"You're just like me, aren't you? Gabriel told us that he had seen this before, and it was you, wasn't it?" I question.

He stays silent, avoiding an answer by getting out of the car and then walking to the front door instead.

Rushing out of the car, I meet him right as Michael opens the door. He glances between us in question for a moment before stepping to the side to let us pass.

Without a word, Marcus and I walk inside and then stop in the living room, where Gabriel stands on his feet.

"Why are you here, Marcus?" Gabriel snarls as his wings begin to unfold.

I'm forced to shield my eyes as a blinding white light engulfs the room.

"Enough, Gabriel, I'm here for her, and you know why. I've been watching her for quite some time." Marcus then sighs as he looks over to me. "Put away the wings, Gabe. I'm here to talk and to ask for your protection."

"Why would you need our protection, Marcus? Angels fear you." Michael asks while stepping next to us.

He looks us both over before turning his full attention to Marcus.

"As far as most think, I've been dead for centuries, Michael. I'm in danger now because of her." Marcus replies while pointing to me.

My jaw drops.

"Why are you in danger because of me?" I ask dumbly.

"Because you and I are the same if we were to have children…well, you can see where I'm heading, right?" Marcus explains while rubbing the back of his neck uncomfortably.

"They would be just like us?" I question.

Gabriel, Marcus, and Michael nod.

"Yes, but they would have an abundance of powers. They would be full-blooded angels too." Gabriel replies as he sits on the couch before placing his head in his hands.

"You should be as far away from her as possible, Marcus. What were you thinking by coming here?" Michael questions.

"I felt a pull to her even before she turned. I've been watching her, but I never once thought that this was why I felt that pull." Marcus rubs the back of his neck again nervously before continuing. "I'm here because it actually hurts to be away from her."

"It physically hurts you?" Gabriel asks as he lifts his head with a look of disbelief.

"I've never felt a pain like it in my entire life, Gabriel. I would rather be anywhere but here, but I seem to have no choice in this matter." Marcus answers.

I ball my hands into fists. His confession hurt. I didn't understand why since I had just met him, but it hurt.

"What could it all mean?" Dad questions softly.

Gabriel's head lifts when we hear a knock on the front door.

All eyes turn to me as if I would know who was on the other side. I shrug and then walk slowly over to the door.

Peeking out the side window, I spot Mason standing on the front porch.

I turn to my dad and the others with a growing blush. I could only think of the words he had spoken to me earlier.

"Who is it, Piper?" Dad questions as he moves over to the door.

He peeks out and then curses before rushing to Gabriel's side. Then, in a flash of bright light, Gabriel disappears.

Marcus pushes past me and opens the door for Mason to come in.

Mason rushes over to me before grabbing me into an abrupt hug.

"Are you alright, Piper?" He asks softly, leaning back slightly to study my eyes.

I nod in response.

Leaning down closer to my ear, his breath washes over my neck. I shiver as he begins to whisper so only I can hear him. "Don't trust that guy, Marcus, Babe. I've known him awhile, and he's not good for you."

I pull back to look into his eyes questioningly.

His eyes only beg me to listen to him. So instead of pushing for an explanation, I give him a slight nod.

His lips form a grin before he turns his attention to Marcus.

"Can we talk somewhere alone, Marcus?" He then growls out.

Marcus grins widely as he nods. He then gestures outside while moving towards the door as Mason follows.

The door slams shut, and I rush over to it, placing my ear against it to listen in on their conversation.

Dad comes over to my side and shakes his head in disapproval.

I shrug, and he leans down to whisper into my ear. "Not every conversation is meant for your ears, Piper. This one is, but don't be shocked when you uncover secrets." He whispers cryptically before walking away.

Placing my ear to the door once more, I listen closely as Marcus and Mason begin to growl out at each other.

"I told you to stay away from her, Marcus. She's mine." Mason starts.

"That's where you're wrong, Mason, the girl is very much mine, and I faintly remember telling you to stay away," Marcus replies.

"What would you want with her, Marcus? She's only human?" Mason growls out in frustration.

Both go silent for a while until Marcus finally speaks.

"I feel drawn to her, Mason. I never thought that anyone would snatch my attention in my life, but she has." He confesses while avoiding telling Mason the whole truth.

"Christ, I fell for her the moment I saw her standing outside her house for the first time." Mason pauses a moment before continuing. "I don't want to fight with you, Marcus, but I want her with every fiber of my being. Hell, you could tear out my wings, and I'd still want her, and only her."

I back away from the door in shock. Did I hear him right? He had wings? That could only mean one thing.

Mason must be an angel.

What I didn't understand, though, is why he thought I was a human, and no one seemed to be correcting him.

"I told you that some secrets are shocking, Piper," Michael states as he walks back in, looking down at me with worry.

I stand to my feet and then pull him into another room. I needed answers, and I needed them now.

"Why doesn't he know what I am?" I ask.

"Gabriel doesn't want his sons involved in our world, Piper. I don't know how Mason knows of Marcus, and I'm sure Gabriel would be shocked, but we have to keep him in the dark about what you are. He can't find out. Not yet, at least." He explains gently.

"So, neither Mason nor Joel knows what's happening around them?" I ask, and he nods. "How do I act around them now, Dad? I don't want to lie to Mason; I like him." I confess.

"We'll figure this all out, Sweetheart, but for now, just keep your secret hidden from him." Rubbing the back of his neck, he continues. "It would be best for you to get to know Marcus anyway. He would be good to you, and he could teach you better than any of us. He knows what you're going through."

"I'm not getting a choice in this, am I?" I ask while searching my father's eyes.

He sighs sadly, giving me my answer.

"You do have a choice, Piper. I'm just trying to steer you in the right direction. I wish things in our world gave you more freedoms, but they don't." He tries to explain.

I nod even as I grit my teeth together.

"I need to go out for a bit. I'll be back later." I clip out as I stomp towards the front door.

"Just be careful, Piper." He commands softly.

I nod and open the door before I storm between a shocked Mason and Marcus.

They both watch as I rush past them and into the garage.

Coming to an abrupt stop, I curse, remembering that Cam had my bike, before glancing around, wondering what I should do.

Just as I'm about to return to the house, I hear my bike's engine coming down the road.

I grin and then meet Cam in the driveway.

He watches me carefully as I place my helmet over my head and then hop on the bike just as he gets off.

"What's wrong?" He asks quietly.

I raise the visor to look at him. "I just need to be alone with my thoughts for a bit. I'll return soon, Cam." I answer simply, not wanting to disclose why I was really leaving.

His eyes narrow, seeing through my lie, but thankful he doesn't question me further. Instead, he only nods before turning and walking to the porch where Mason and Marcus are still standing, watching me.

Marcus steps down the steps slowly while shaking his head for me not to go.

He looks back to Cam and Mason before turning back to me. '*Please, don't leave,*' he mouths with fear showing clearly in his eyes.

Even though I knew it would hurt him, I had to leave. I couldn't stay around for another moment. I had to get away from this, from them, so I could collect my thoughts and sort through them.

Stepping closer, his eyes still plead for me to stay, but I shake my head once more. This time he stops before his head bows in defeat, knowing that he wouldn't be able to stop me.

As his head rises again, I mouth to him, '*I won't go far.*'

He nods his head once before walking backward, back to the house.

Starting the bike, I flip down my visor and then take off.

Pulling out onto the road, I speed as fast as possible through the town and towards the park where I could fly and find a little peace to relax.

It was a place where I could sort out the information I had just learned too.

The freedom to fly was really the only thing left that couldn't be taken away from me.

Reaching the park, I hop off my bike before wandering over to the bench that overlooked a large lake.

It was beautiful, with the stars reflecting down onto the water.

I sit there staring at the small waves of water as I allow my thoughts to roam over the last few days. It felt as if a lifetime had been packed into just a few short days.

A branch snaps behind me, and I jump to my feet in alarm.

Marcus holds his hands up, and I curse to myself before I sit back down.

He sits next to me and sighs while leaning forward, placing his elbows on his knees.

"I know you wanted your space, but you went too far, and it started to hurt." He pauses to look up at me. "I'm sorry."

"You shouldn't be the one who's sorry, Marcus. I went farther than I thought I would, even though I knew you'd be in pain. If anyone should be sorry, it's me." I sigh roughly while turning my face to look directly up at the stars.

"I'm sorry that you're stuck with this bond, or whatever it is. I know you don't want to be around me. It would be smart to stay away, though. All I seem to do is break hearts." I add sadly.

"I'm not just here because of the bond. I've been interested in you for as long as you have been alive." He confesses.

"Why?" I ask while turning my attention back to him.

He sighs softly before speaking. "Because angels don't die easily, and when it comes to our race, it's made up of males only, except for you now. I wanted to find someone that

I could spend an eternity with, not just someone I would have to watch eventually die. I want more from this life."

"All I ever wanted was to be normal, Marcus. But, unfortunately, we don't always get what we want." I growl out harshly while standing to my feet.

I look around to make sure no one else had appeared before allowing my wings to unfold, thankful for not having to take off my shirt since it was a halter top.

I quickly make a mental note to wear these kinds of shirts more often.

Glancing back, I watch as Marcus shucks off his shirt, revealing cut abs.

I sigh inwardly as I roll my eyes. Of course, he would be attractive. I then groan softly as his wings fan out, making him even more appealing.

His wingspan was nearly twice as big as mine was, and with the stars causing his red feathers to shimmer in the light, it was truly an amazing sight to witness.

Grinning, he comes over to me before running his hands along my wings.

I shiver involuntarily and close my eyes, both enjoying his touch and hating it.

"Your wings are gorgeous, Piper." He whispers into my ear.

His wings press forward against mine, and I find myself leaning back into his embrace.

"Can I taste your blood?" He asks softly.

I find myself nodding as I tilt my head slightly to give him better access.

His lips trail across my neck, and I wait for the bite, but instead of him biting me, his lips leave my skin before he brings my wrist up to his mouth.

I turn and watch as his fangs descend. He smiles softly before biting into my skin. His eyes then close as his tongue begins lapping up my blood.

All too soon, he pulls away after licking the punctures closed on my wrist. I cradle it to myself as I rub at it absently.

"Marcus, how do you know Mason?" I ask softly.

"We've known each other for a while now. We met here, actually." He answers as he runs his hands through his hair. "I had come here before you, Hannah, and your mom moved. I wanted to see how safe it was for you in this town, and I unexpectedly ran into him. We fought, but when he realized just how dangerous of an angel that I was, he quickly backed down."

"You didn't hurt him, did you?" I inquire curiously.

"No, I haven't hurt anyone who didn't deserve it. I stick to a code that Gabriel and I set into place for angels like us. We don't kill unless it's necessary." He replies.

"I don't want to have to kill anyone at all, Marcus," I whisper.

He releases a breath while moving closer to me. "You won't have to with me here. I will take care of you, Piper."

I nod as I bow my head.

He wraps his arms gently around me, and I lean my head against his chest.

"Mason really likes you, you know?" Marcus blurts after a few minutes of silence.

I smile and look up at him.

"Yes, I know, and I like him too." I sigh and shake my head roughly. "I still have feelings for his brother Joel though. I really thought what I had felt for him was real, but it was nothing more than a lie."

"You mean that guy that made you cry at the club?" He asks, and I nod as I look to the side, willing myself not to shed another tear. "I'm sorry, Sweetheart."

"Don't be sorry… it's just that he was the first guy that I ever really gave my attention to. I was really hoping that it would turn into something good." I confess as I will my wings away while stepping back from Marcus's embrace.

I bow my head and turn to face the lake once more.

"You'll find what you're looking for, Piper. Sometimes what you're looking for is right in front of you." He states as he steps up beside me.

"I want to believe that, but it's hard to do when something else holds my attention," I reply while bowing my head.

Marcus steps forward, turning in front of me before he raises my chin with his hand.

He leans in, and just when I think he's about to kiss me, he curses and then steps back abruptly.

His wings quickly fold away as he takes another step away from me.

"Marcus, what is it?" I ask, almost in a panic.

He only shakes his head.

"Marcus, what are you doing here with her?" Mason suddenly yells out in anger from behind me.

I turn my face to see him storming his way over toward us.

"I just wanted to make sure that she was alright, Mason," Marcus answers simply.

Mason steps right up behind me and wraps his arms around my waist.

It almost felt as if he was claiming me, which I guess in a sense he was since Marcus takes yet another step back.

"Stay away from her, Marcus. You're no good for her." Mason growls in warning.

I stare at Marcus as he bows his head and then nods as he frowns. "You're right, Mason. I probably wouldn't be any good for her."

Standing there in shock, I continue to watch him.

What was he doing? Just moments ago, he had just been telling me that we would be good together, and now he was saying that he wouldn't be good for me. His back and forth was making my head ache with confusion.

Turning me in his arms, Mason looks deep into my eyes. "Are you alright? He didn't hurt you in any way, did he?"

A soft wind hits my back suddenly, and when Mason's eyes glance behind me for a brief second, I realize that Marcus had left.

"I'm fine. Marcus was just worried about me." I answer softly and then look behind me to where Marcus should have still been.

I look all around, playing my part of being human, before looking back at Mason curiously.

"Where did he go?" I question.

"He left," Mason replies while placing his hand against my cheek. "We should get you home. It's getting late, and I'm sure your mom and sister will be worried about you."

"Yeah, I guess we should get back," I answer softly while looking into his eyes.

Leaning down, his lips slowly brush over mine, testing me, teasing me. I grin before wrapping a hand around the back of his neck, pulling him closer for a kiss.

His lips grin against mine as they continue to move.

After a few passion-filled minutes, Mason pulls away and grins wider as he pants for his breath.

"Let's get you back home, Piper." He suggests with another kiss.

I nod before pulling away this time.

"I just need a few more minutes to myself, if you don't mind. I'll let you know when I make it home, okay?" I insist.

He frowns. "Are you sure? I really don't like leaving you here alone."

"I'll be fine, Mason. I'm not just some harmless little girl." I smile and walk over to my bike before pulling a handgun from a compartment under the seat.

He grins and then nods to me as he takes the gun from my hands, inspecting it closely before handing it back.

"Alright, I'll leave you, but promise me if anything happens, you will call me, okay?" He insists.

"I will," I promise while placing the gun back into my bike.

He turns and begins walking down the road, turning back only once to give me a wide grin. I smile back and touch my lips absently, thinking about our kiss.

It had been amazing, and what I had with him felt natural. It wasn't like being with Joel at all, and I was happy with that.

I continue to watch Mason's back until he fades into the distance before I turn back to the water and sigh as I allow my wings to unfold once more.

It felt so good just to be myself in this place.

I yelp in surprise as hands circle my waist from behind. I quickly sense that they are Marcus's and lean back into him.

His lips touch my neck, and he sighs softly against my skin.

Being with him like this felt right too, but I didn't want him like I wanted Mason.

"I thought he would never leave," Marcus whispers in my ear, causing me to shiver.

"Now, we can finally fly." He laughs as his breath fans out over my skin before he takes a step back with his hands still holding my hips.

Just as I'm about to take flight, a sharp pain washes through my body, and I cry out.

Marcus falls with me to our knees, never letting me go.

I cry out as the pain washes through me over and over. I had hoped that I was past this, but I guess that was just a useless wish.

"Damn it; he couldn't have just stayed away." Marcus curses. "Piper, Sweetheart, can you fold your wings away? Mason is coming back. He must have heard you cry out."

I shake my head. "I can't."

I couldn't will them away, not while I was in so much pain.

"What the hell are you doing to her, Marcus?" Mason growls out.

"This is not the time, Mason; just go away," Marcus commands.

"I will kill you, Marcus. Get your hands off of her, now." Mason snarls out, coming closer.

"Mason, just listen to me. I'm not hurting her, I would never hurt Piper, but if you don't leave, she will end up hurting you." Marcus warns before the pain fades and the thirst takes over, causing my fangs to descend.

Marcus's arms hold me tightly as I try to fight against him.

I could smell Mason's blood pumping through his body, and I wanted nothing more than to taste it on my tongue.

"What the hell are you talking…?" Mason trails off as he comes to stand in front of us.

His eyes go wide before glancing questioningly at Marcus.

"Did you do this to her?" He snaps as his hands ball into fists.

"No, I did not; she was born this way, Mason, just like I was." Marcus states before he grunts out as I shove my elbow into his stomach. "Leave now, Mason. She wants your blood and might kill you if she gets a hold of you. She won't know any better."

"She can have my blood if it's what she needs, Marcus," Mason answers before dropping to his knees in front of us.

"I'm not going to be able to stop you, am I?" Marcus questions, and Mason shakes his head.

With one well-placed elbow to Marcus's stomach, he loosens his grip, and I shove away from his arms before pouncing on Mason.

His eyes go wide with fear just before I sink my fangs deep into his neck.

Hands grab me from behind relentlessly, trying to pry me away from Mason's sweet blood.

"Piper, you must stop," Marcus growls in my ear. "You'll kill him if you don't."

Not listening, I spread my wings, shielding us away from Marcus.

I just want to be left alone.

"Mason, tell her. Stop her." Marcus demands but curses when Mason doesn't answer.

His heartbeat was quickly becoming faint.

Without warning, Marcus roughly grabs my wings as I fight to keep a hold of Mason. This time he successfully rips me away before sinking his fangs into my neck.

He forces his wrist into my mouth, and I bite down, tasting his blood.

Groaning with pleasure, I close my eyes.

As his wrist leaves my mouth a few moments later, I drop to the ground, but before my eyes flutter shut, I watch Cam fly down before kneeling next to Mason's lifeless body.

"What the hell happened, Marcus?" He growls just before I pass out.

Chapter Seven

Lying back in my bed, I run the events of the night before in my head.

I had almost killed Mason.

The simple fact was that I had no control over myself. I was a danger to everyone around me, and Marcus was the only one who could stop me.

My dad had been right when he said I should become closer to him; he knew that no one else would be able to take care of me like Marcus could.

He also knew that I would end up killing someone if I didn't gain control.

A tear slips from my eye as I recall Mason's lifeless body. I had wanted something special between us, but not if it would cost him his life.

We had been lucky this time, but I would probably kill someone the next time. I would probably kill Mason.

I knew what I had to do, but it killed me to even think of it. It wasn't fair. I was falling in love with him, and it wasn't fair that I would now have to give him up.

Hannah knocks on my open door before coming in to sit next to me on my bed. Wordlessly she takes my hand in hers, giving me the support and comfort I needed so badly.

"Everything will work out the way it should, Piper." She whispers, looking beyond her age.

I nod as another tear slips from my eye.

I hoped that she was right.

And I hoped that my life wouldn't be full of heartbreak.

"Are you coming to school with us today?" She then questions while forcing herself to smile.

"You should come with us, Sis. It would do you some good to get out of this room." Cam urges as he walks into my room, with Marcus following close behind.

Giving my hand one last squeeze, Hannah stands to her feet and then shyly walks past the two boys to exit through the door.

"How's Mason?" I ask, turning my attention to Cam, not wanting to talk with Marcus right now.

I don't know how or why, but something had changed between us when he had bitten my neck.

"He's better, still a bit weak, but he'll be just fine." Cam answers while rubbing the back of his neck as he glances over to Marcus before sighing loudly. "He wants to see you, Piper."

"I almost killed him. So why would he want to see me?" I question while sitting up in bed.

"He loves you, Piper. Can't you see that?" Cam asks while glancing at me and then at Marcus, who had yet to take his eyes off me.

"He should hate me," I whisper and then laugh sadly. "I bet Gabriel does; I broke his one rule. I exposed our world to Mason."

"Gabriel is mad, but he isn't mad at you. He's mad at everything in general." Cam replies.

"Is it really safe for me to even be at school?" I ask, changing the subject.

"I will be there with you," Marcus answers this time.

The sound of his voice alone causes me to shiver. It was like music to my ears, the beat that my heart pounded to.

"Cam, can you give us a few minutes to talk alone?" I insist softly.

He nods before walking out of the room, shutting the door behind him, and leaving Marcus and me alone.

In one swift move, Marcus lands on top of me on my bed. He places one hand behind my head and his other on my hip.

His mouth quickly descends, and I moan as his tongue dances with mine.

It was almost an uncontrollable urge to be closer to him, and soon I find myself ripping his shirt away from his body as he, too, rips mine away.

His mouth trails hungrily down my neck.

I turn my head just as Cam walks back into the room, his eyes going wide before he covers them with his hand.

"Guys, what the hell are you doing?" He asks.

"She's mine," Marcus growls as he turns red eyes on Cam while his body tenses above me, ready for a fight.

Again, I watch as Cam's arm drops to reveal his wide, shocked eyes.

Marcus lets out a frightening snarl, and Cam backs away and then out the door with his hands raised high in surrender.

Once the door shuts again, Marcus nuzzles his face back into my neck while his body relaxes from its tense position above me.

My mind becomes fuzzy as he caresses my skin with his hands and lips.

It isn't until I hear my father's voice that I come back out of the fog in my mind.

"Marcus, you need to gain control of yourself now." He commands gruffly.

"She. Is. Mine." He snarls back possessively as his wings unfold to cover us.

"What's going on?" Gabriel's voice rings out, causing Marcus to growl as his lips grace my skin.

"I don't know, Gabe. You know more about Marcus than anyone. You tell us what he's doing with my daughter." Michael yells out in anger.

"He spoke of a bond earlier, and if my books were right, then he's her mate, and it appears that he's trying to make her his. So, he must feel some sort of threat to their bond." Gabriel answers quickly.

Michael curses as something smashes against the wall.

"Can we stop this before they do something stupid? Piper won't want this, not like this," Cam states helplessly.

"The only way to stop this is to know who or what the threat is, and we don't have a clue of who or what that threat could possibly be." Gabriel answers in frustration.

"Yes, we do. It's Mason; he has to be the only threat. He loves Piper." Cam states loudly, causing Marcus to let out another angry snarl.

"Go get him now, Cam," Michael commands before they leave the room.

"Marcus, please stop for a minute," I whisper while placing my hands on his smooth chest.

He grunts in response before stopping to look me in the eyes. His deep red eyes soften, and I smile.

"I don't want to stop. I need you. I want you." He growls softly.

"I know you do, but we can't do this like this, Marcus." I reason with him.

Placing his forehead against mine, he nods.

"I'm not going to lose you to him, am I?" He whispers, his voice pleading for me to say no.

"You won't lose me, Marcus. Last night opened my eyes. I could have killed him, and I don't want that." I sigh softly. "The only way to keep everyone safe is to let him go. So, I'll be yours and yours alone, Marcus."

"You would really give him up for me?" He questions seriously.

I nod. I loved Mason and would do anything for him, even if it meant breaking our hearts to keep him safe.

Closing his eyes, Marcus sighs in relief. His wings quickly fold away, exposing us to my father, Cam, Gabriel, and Mason, who had returned without us noticing.

I groan as I try and fail to cover myself.

Climbing off and standing to his feet, Marcus tries to hide me the best he can as I pull on my torn shirt. I quickly tie it, so it covers as much as possible before standing to my feet next to Marcus.

"Please, tell me that you didn't...." Michael trails off.

"We didn't. I stopped him, and we talked things over." I answer and watch as they all visibly release deep breaths of relief.

"I'll be downstairs when you're ready to go, Piper," Marcus whispers before kissing my cheek.

"Gabriel, Michael, we have much to discuss, so let's leave Mason and Piper alone to talk." Marcus insists.

Both older angels nod in agreement before following him out of the room.

"If you need me, I'll be right outside the door, Piper," Cam states while looking between Mason and me before he leaves, shutting the door behind him.

"Mason, I'm sorry…." I trail off as he steps closer and places his finger against my lips.

"Don't say it, please, don't say that you're doing this for me. I refuse to lose you just because you're scared of hurting me." He pleads before smashing his lips against mine.

I'm helpless against him.

My feelings for him overruled my logic. I know it was wrong to kiss Mason back, but I do with as much passion as I could muster.

Pulling back moments later, I smile sadly. I knew that, in the end, breaking both of our hearts was the only way to fix this.

"We can't do this anymore, Mason. I love you, but we can never be. I'm too dangerous to be around." I whisper, trying to make him understand.

"You will gain control, and when you do, then we can have our chance. Just promise me that you won't give yourself to him fully." Mason compromises.

I nod, knowing that it would be next to impossible to stop Marcus the next time he felt threatened in any way. I had barely gotten him to stop this time.

With one last soft kiss, I stand in place as Mason leaves me alone in my room.

Touching my fingers to my lips, I close my eyes.

I didn't know how I would manage to keep my heart from breaking.

After years of keeping my heart hidden, I didn't understand how one man had snatched it from me in such a short amount of time.

"Are you about ready to go, Piper?" Cam's voice calls out from the other side of the door.

"Yeah, I'll be out in just a minute," I reply before rushing around my room to get ready.

A few moments later, Marcus walks back into my room without knocking. I quickly slip on my boots and stand to my feet.

His eyes roam over my body as he licks his lips with hunger.

Walking up to him, I place my hands against his chest and tilt my head to the side, knowing just what he needed. He needed to feel me; he needed to be reassured that I was still his, and he needed this as a way to claim me.

His lips barely trail against my neck before his fangs gently pierce my skin. His hands grip my hips tightly as his tongue laps up my blood.

Taking one last pull of blood, he licks the wounds closed and then nuzzles his nose into my neck.

"You're mine, don't ever forget that." He whispers before pulling away.

I nod as he takes my hand in his before leading me downstairs.

My mom kisses my cheek before handing me two lunches as we then head out of the house.

Holding out his hand, Cam takes the lunches before hopping into Mason's truck.

I watch them, wondering when they had become friends, as Marcus hops on my bike and pats the back for me to get on.

Mason frowns in our direction and then looks away as I climb onto the back of the bike before I wrap my arms around Marcus.

I could almost feel his heart breaking.

Mine was.

I just had to keep this up until I gained control, and then I would be free to be with Mason. At least, that's what I kept telling myself.

Deep down, though, I knew that we would never be.

Chapter Eight

Walking into the lunchroom after an exhausting morning of school was almost painful, to say the least. Everyone watched as Marcus and I walked in.

Every girl in the room hated me, and every guy hated him.

I hated being in the spotlight like that, but Marcus absolutely adored it.

For me, it was the fact that the girls all watched him. I hated that they all wanted him for themselves.

I know I shouldn't have felt that way, but I did.

Sitting in a chair at an empty table, I wait for Cam, Mason, and Marcus to join me.

They had gone through the lunch line in order to get us food since Cam and Mason had eaten our lunches on the way to school.

"Where have you been hiding?" Beth huffs out while sitting down next to me.

"It's been a crazy week, Beth. I'll have to tell you about it all later." I answer, hoping that it would suffice.

"You better." She warns with a smile.

I smile back and feel the first bit of relief wash over me since I had come to this little town.

Beth was a good person and a good friend.

When she looks past me, and her eyes widen, I knew just who she had seen. I feel his presence as he moves closer.

Beth leans in closer while still watching him from over my shoulder.

"Who is he? He's ten degrees of hotness." She whispers and then coughs as Marcus, Cam, and Mason sit with us at the table.

Marcus's hand reaches out to shake Beth's hand, and I can't help but giggle when she blushes.

"I'm Marcus, and thank you for the compliment. I don't think I've ever heard anyone call me ten degrees of hotness before." He chuckles as her blush deepens.

Finally taking his hand in hers, she gives him a shy shake before quickly pulling her hand back.

"I'm Beth." She whispers.

"Oh, so this is your best friend that you told me about." Marcus looks at me.

I nod. I hadn't said a word about her, but it was sweet of him to make her feel special.

"You actually told him about me?" Beth asks, surprised.

"Of course I did. You are my best friend, after all, aren't you?" I question, causing her eyes to light up as she nods.

For a moment, I wonder if she had ever had a best friend.

Pushing a tray between us, Marcus nods towards it, letting me know that I could take whatever I wanted first.

I grab a red apple, promptly taking a big bite of it to avoid any more conversation.

It wasn't the fact that I didn't want to talk, but I was tired of telling people who Marcus was and why he was following me around like a lost puppy dog.

On top of that, I would then have to explain why a girl like me would break up with someone like Cam.

On and on the list went for the things that I had to explain to the most random people today. I was mentally exhausted, and I was ready for the day just to be over already.

"Oh, no, anyone but them," Beth whispers, catching my attention.

I glance in the direction she's looking and curse my luck.

Jayden, Sara, and Sasha were headed our way.

Jayden, of course, was targeting Mason, Sara was looking at her sister, and Sasha had her eyes pinned on Marcus.

I had a sudden feeling this was going to turn into an even rougher day.

"Why aren't any of them looking at me? I'm hot, too, right?" Cam pouts, causing me to bark out in laughter.

"Of course you are, Cam, but you should be happy that none of them have targeted you," I answer while giggling.

"Hey, Mason, I've missed you." Jayden croons as she forces herself into his lap.

My jaw clenches when he smiles at her sweetly.

"Missed you too, Jayden." He whispers back.

"And who might you be?" Sasha asks while sliding herself onto Marcus's lap.

He grins widely and wraps his arm around her back.

"I'm Marcus, and what's your name, beautiful?" He replies.

That was the last straw. I couldn't take anymore.

I stand from my seat before rushing out of the lunchroom. I didn't want to see them acting like that anymore. And what happened to Marcus being my boyfriend at school; that was definitely not how a boyfriend acted.

He was supposed to be mine.

Running down the hall with tears begging to fall from my eyes, I run straight into a pair of strong arms.

I look up to see Joel looking down at me as my tears begin to pour from my eyes and down my cheeks.

This whole day had been a mistake.

I should have just stayed home.

"What's wrong, Piper? Who made you cry?" He asks, surprising me.

"Why are you suddenly being so nice to me, Joel?" I question with a hiccup as I continue to cry.

He looks away, ashamed for a moment.

"I didn't know what I know now, Piper. I'm sorry for what I said and did." He sighs before looking me directly in the eyes. "Tell me, who made my girl cry?"

"It's no use to tell you. I'm sure it will be all over the school that I ran away and let those horrible girls flaunt themselves all over my boyfriend." I explain as I shake my head, angry with myself, as I wipe away my tears. "I even left poor Beth in there to deal with it all by herself."

"You mean to tell me that my brother and Marcus are both the cause of your crying and that they are in there now letting those…." He trails off for a moment as his face turns red with anger.

"I'm going to kick both of them until they bleed." He then growls out.

Placing my hand on his arm to stop him from doing something foolish, I grin while coming up with a better plan.

"How about we get them back in a better way, Joel? Are you up for a little acting?" I ask.

His eyes light up with mischievous intent.

"You know I'm up for anything, Sweetheart." He answers before I begin whispering my plan into his ear.

After I finish telling him my plan, he steps back to look at me with a raised brow.

"Seriously, you want me to get my butt kicked, don't you?" He laughs even as he agrees to my plan.

"You owe me, Joel, and this is me getting back at your brother and my supposed boyfriend. They both deserve to feel a bit of jealousy." I answer, determined to make them pay.

"Jealousy isn't even going to cross their minds, Piper. On the contrary, they're going to be downright ticked off." Joel states seriously and then mock gasps placing his hand over his heart. "They might even try to kill me for this, Piper. Think of all the lonely girls I'll leave behind."

"Oh, shut up. You know you love this plan." I laugh as I take his hand and wrap it around my waist.

"Yup, I love this plan already." He chuckles before we head back to the lunchroom together.

I grit my teeth seeing Sasha and Jayden still sitting on Marcus's and Mason's laps. Cam, on the other hand, I didn't mind seeing him in a debate between Sara and Beth.

As Joel and I approach the table, all eyes turn to us.

Both Mason's and Marcus's jaws tick with anger when they spot where Joel's hand lies on my exposed hip.

Sitting down in the seat that I had just vacated, Joel taps his lap for me to sit. I grin widely as I sit and then lean back against his chest as his hands hold onto my upper thighs.

Sasha scowls at me. "Are you and Joel back together then, Piper?"

I nod. "Yes, we are, so you're welcome to have my leftovers. They weren't as fun as Joel is anyway." I answer smugly.

Sasha and Jayden both gasp in shock. I had just made them both out to be second-rate.

I laugh at their faces as they glance around at everyone watching us in the lunchroom. It was like watching an episode of a soap opera.

Every eye was on us, even the teachers.

Sliding off both Mason's and Marcus's laps, both girls give me the dirtiest looks they could manage before looking at Sara.

"Let's go, Sara. I don't want to be seen around Piper, the whore." Jayden bites out menacingly.

Sara quickly gets up and follows them as they all rush out of the lunchroom in a huff.

Joel tickles my sides, and I laugh, catching Mason's and Marcus's full attention.

Playing his part, Joel nuzzles my neck. "Think about the lonely girls I'm going to leave behind when they kill me, Piper." He whispers, causing me to giggle again.

"What in the hell do you think you're doing, Piper?" Marcus growls so only we can hear him.

"I could have just asked you the same thing, Marcus," I reply before turning from him to kiss Joel.

I know I was playing with fire, but at the moment, I didn't care. I didn't deserve to have to watch as another girl had her hands on him.

"That's it; I'm done. I'm leaving." Marcus states while standing on his feet. "I don't want to be around you if this is how you're going to act, Piper. That girl was right; you are a whore."

"And you're an absolute idiot, Marcus," Joel states quietly as we watch Marcus leave.

"I'm leaving too. I can't stand seeing you with my brother again, Piper." Mason growls as he stands to his feet and then walks away too.

"What idiots." Cam agrees with Joel. "They're both idiots."

"I think we may have gone too far with the payback, Sweetheart." Joel mumbles.

"No, no, you didn't. They were being horrible to you, Piper, and they deserved that for making you cry." Beth responds fiercely.

"You were crying?" Cam asks, and I nod along with Joel.

"Yeah, she ran into me in the hall crying because of them," Joel explains.

"Just leave them be; then, if they come back, they better be sorry, but if they don't, we will make them sorry for making you cry, Sis," Cam promises.

"Wait, back this train up a minute. Did you just call her Sis?" Beth exclaims while looking directly at Cam.

"As I said, Beth, I have a lot of explaining to do. And, yes, he's my half-brother." I answer her.

"You have a ton to explain, Piper, but for now, just let them boys run off. You'll get them back. They would be stupid not to come back to you." Beth sighs.

****

Leaving the lunchroom when the bell rings, Joel holds me back while Cam and Beth walk off.

"Are you going to be alright?" He asks softly.

"I'll be fine, Joel. I'm a big girl. I can handle them." I lie.

In all honesty, I didn't know if I could handle one of them, let alone both of them.

"If you need me, just run, and I'll let you slam into me, okay?" Joel teases, causing me to laugh abruptly.

I nod." Thank you, Joel."

"You're welcome, Piper." He replies.

We then walk out of the lunchroom together and go our separate ways.

Walking to my class, I sigh roughly. I just couldn't wait for this horrible day to be over.

How had things gotten so crazy in such a short time?

It felt like just yesterday that I was sitting in the car wondering how my mom, sister, and I were going to make it in this town.

Chapter Nine

Thankfully when Marcus left, he had left me with my bike to get home on. The keys for it had been hanging in my locker, along with my helmet.

Sighing loudly, I walk out to the parking lot and hop on my bike.

I wait as Joel comes out before he walks over to me.

"Are you going straight home?" He asks, and I nod. "I'll follow you home then, okay?" I nod again and then slide on my helmet.

I watch as he gets into his car. Moments later, the engine roars to life.

With a nod of his head, I start my bike and then take off. He pulls in behind me, and I force myself to keep slow so he can follow me.

He was just worried about me.

And I must admit, it was nice to have someone worry about me.

I was also glad that because of his worry, I wasn't rushing home to who knew what. I could have been rushing home to find out that Marcus had really left me for good.

It was a scary feeling.

Maybe I had gone too far, but he shouldn't have let Sasha anywhere near him.

In hindsight, we were both in the wrong, and if he were man enough to actually apologize, then I would too.

As we get closer to our houses, my stomach twists in knots, not knowing what I was coming home to.

Pulling into my driveway, I notice Mason's truck in his and sigh in relief. They both must have come back together.

Parking my bike, I take off my helmet and then quickly rush into the house, wanting to see Marcus and talk to him.

I'm disappointed when I run from room to room, and he's nowhere to be found.

My heart sinks.

I must have really made him leave me.

"Piper, who are you looking for?" Mom asks, coming out from the kitchen.

"Have you seen Marcus, Mom?" I ask quietly.

She shakes her head, and my heart sinks. "No, Sweetie, I haven't seen him since you two left for school this morning."

"He really left then," I whisper as I sit down on the steps, feeling rejected. "I can't believe he left me."

"What happened, Piper? Tell me what happened." Mom pleads as she kneels in front of me.

"I did something foolish to get back at Marcus and Mason. As a result, they both left school angry." I confess as tears pool in my eyes. "Marcus said he was done with me when he left." I whimper as my tears begin to fall. "I don't think he's coming back."

Wrapping her arms around me, my mom gives me the comfort only a mother could provide.

"Everything will work out the way it should, Piper." She croons.

I laugh sadly. "That's the second time someone's told me that today."

Only things weren't working out in my favor, and I had been left with a broken heart.

"I've got to finish dinner, Piper. Your father will be coming home in a bit. Will you be okay?" Mom asks.

I nod and wipe the few tears that had escaped from my face with the back of my hands before she stands to her feet and reluctantly walks away.

I sit on the steps staring at the door waiting, waiting for Marcus or even Mason to walk through the door.

I jump up as the door opens, but my face falls when Hannah walks in.

She looks at me sadly, already knowing my question. "I haven't seen him, Piper. I'm sorry."

Hannah sits next to me, taking my hand in hers as we wait together.

I'm glad she's by my side when Michael comes through the door shaking his head in anger and disappointment.

"I'm just going to go." Hannah jumps up quickly, leaving my father and me alone.

"Piper, how could you be so stupid." He yells out.

"How could I be so stupid? Why are you even asking that when you should be asking about what he did to me? You shouldn't be mad at me; you should be mad at him." I yell back as tears begin to stream freely down my cheeks.

"I know what he did, but what you did was worse, Piper." He answers.

My jaw drops for a moment before my anger bubbles over.

"He let her put her hands on him. She had her hands on what's mine, and you have the nerve to say what I did was worse. I know you want me to be a good girl and listen to you and to whoever you decide is good for me, but I'm not going to sit around and be treated that way." I growl while poking my finger against his chest roughly.

"I should be a prize to be won. Any man, angel or not, should have to work to keep me." I spit out before I shove him and then walk out the front door.

I push my way past Cam and Joel, who tries his hardest to stop me, ignoring them as they follow me while I walk around the house into the backyard.

"Don't do it, Piper, you're only going to regret it," Joel yells, somehow knowing what I was planning on doing.

"Who the hell cares, Joel? If it makes me feel anything other than what I feel right now, I will welcome it." I answer as I rip my shirt to allow my wings out.

I look skyward before looking back towards my mom and sister, who were in the back doorway watching me with tears glistening in their eyes.

I didn't care anymore. I just wanted to feel something other than heartbreak.

Pushing off the ground, I take to the air, flying higher than I had ever gone before.

I fly as high as I can before I will my wings away and start my fall back to the ground.

Closing my eyes, I silently pray for death. I was so tired of this life. I was tired of hiding, and I was tired of feeling like I meant nothing.

Falling, I pick up speed and grin.

Cam and Joel both try to catch me, but since I was falling so fast, they could barely keep up.

"If you want me, Marcus, you better save me," I yell out as the ground rapidly grows closer.

If he cared at all, then he would be nearby.

When he doesn't come to save me, I cry out with heartbreak as the ground nears.

Moments before I slam into the ground, I look over at my mother and sister. Michael was thankfully shielding them from seeing my final moments.

I look over to Mason next.

His face registers what I am doing before he runs towards me as fast as he can.

And then Beth steps out from the house, catching my eyes.

Her mouth drops as she spots me.

It's the last thing I see before my body slams full force into the hard and unforgiving ground.

Chapter Ten

"**W**hy would she do this?" I hear Mason ask quietly.

"Seriously, you're actually going to ask that?" Beth screeches. "It's a wonder the poor girl didn't do it sooner. Each and every one of you are to blame for this. From what you have all told me, I'm not surprised that she finally lost it. I bet she felt completely alone."

"And you, did you really think that letting those two bimbos sit on your laps at lunch wouldn't bother her? Did you really think that she would just sit back and let that happen? If you did, then you don't know her at all." She continues to rant.

I loved her for it.

"If there is anyone in this room that actually cares about Piper, it's Joel. He had his heart broken just because you weren't man enough to tell your sons what she actually was. Hell, he even went as far as helping her to make you jealous, Mason. He has been the only one so far that I can see who is mostly innocent in this."

The room goes quiet for a few minutes.

"Is she even going to survive this?" Beth finally asks in a softer tone.

"She should, but it's taking longer for her to heal than it ever has for any of us," Mason replies.

"You've all done this?" My mom gasps.

"We have all wished for death at some point, Helen, and being young; you don't think. You just do the one thing that you think will kill you," Michael answers her gently.

"I've done it twice." Joel chimes in. "Worst two mistakes of my life. The pain from healing is unbearable."

"So, is she's in a lot of pain right now?" Mom asks.

"She probably doesn't feel anything right now, but when she wakes up, she will. She has broken nearly every bone in her body. Even most of her organs have been damaged." Gabriel answers this time.

"She must have gone as high as she could." He mutters softly.

"Cam and I couldn't even catch up with her when she was freefalling," Joel adds.

"Does anyone know where Marcus is?" Michael growls out in frustration.

"I haven't seen or heard from him since we left the school." Mason answers.

"I thought that he couldn't be away from her without being in pain, Gabriel." Michael states.

Gabriel sighs roughly. "He did say that, but I don't know to what point he can handle the pain. It might be just a pinprick of pain or a sharp stabbing pain. Unfortunately, there isn't much written about them, Michael."

"He could help her heal," Cam growls out in anger.

"So can we, son. It will just take more from us to help her," Dad answers softly.

"Why did all of you have to mess up our lives so much? All she ever wanted was to be normal." Hannah cries out abruptly.

I could only imagine the look on her face. It was probably a mix of anger and tears.

"Calm down, Hannah, you know that it's better this way. It's better for Piper to know what she is and to be around others like her. She'll have a chance now." Mom replies softly.

"I will not calm down, Mom. I just watched my sister fall from the sky. I watched her body slam into the ground, and when she should be dead, she's lying on her bed healing. If you expect me to calm down after all of that, then you must be crazy." Hannah shouts hysterically.

"Come on, Hannah, let's take a walk?" Cam suggests.

I imagine him placing a comforting arm around her before leading her from the room.

My poor sister, I could only fathom the nightmares that my stupid stunt would give her. I never thought once about how this would affect them. I had only thought of Marcus and how he must not have wanted me.

It was a selfish stunt.

"Mason, Joel. I want you both out looking for Marcus. We need him here to help her." Gabriel commands.

I listen to their footsteps leave the room, leaving only my parents, Gabriel and Beth.

"Beth, do you need a ride home?" My mom asks.

Beth must answer wordlessly because I listen to their footsteps exit the room next, leaving me alone in the room with only Gabriel and my father.

"She isn't getting any better, Michael," Gabriel whispers moments later.

"I know, but what can we do?" Dad replies, troubled.

"Today is her eighteenth birthday, right?" Gabriel questions.

"Yes, but what does that matter?" Dad inquires.

"I didn't want to say any of this in front of her mother, but if she doesn't recover enough to survive the full change, I'm afraid it will kill her. That's why we need Marcus." Gabriel replies, distressed.

"I never even thought of that, Gabriel." Dad sniffles sadly as his hand slides into mine. "I should have been here for her for all of those years. I've been a horrible father."

"How were you to know you had a daughter, Michael? None of us ever expect a female to be born like us. It's our curse." Gabriel answers with a loud sigh before continuing. "You're here for her now, and that's what matters most."

"I only hope that we can save her, but even if we do manage to save her, what will this life really offer her?" Dad asks quietly, with tears clogging his words.

"With Marcus, she has hope for a future. Hell, even if she chose Mason, she would have a future. I hate to admit that, but I can't deny that my son loves her. Both of my sons do." Gabriel replies.

"Yes, they do, but we must push her towards Marcus, you know that." Michael insists. "She could easily kill any other angel that she comes in contact with. We truly don't know how far her powers will range. Marcus has kept many of his abilities hidden from us."

"What happens when others find out about her?" Dad then asks, changing the subject.

Gabriel lets out a long breath before responding. "Some will beg for death, others will worship her, and others will want her to use against all angels. It will begin a battle of epic proportions if they find out about her."

"It will be the beginning of the end of days, Michael." He adds seriously.

"That's what I'm afraid of. She will have to hide for the rest of her life." Dad sighs sadly.

"She's used to that lifestyle, Michael, and if Marcus returns, he will be able to keep her hidden better than any of us can," Gabriel reassures.

"Do you believe he will return?" Michael questions.

"He will. I am certain of this." Gabriel answers with conviction. "I must go with my sons to search. I will return soon, Michael."

Warmth floats over my exposed skin for a moment before it disappears.

Gabriel was gone.

Even they had tricks up their sleeves that I would never fully understand.

Opening my eyes, I look at my father as pain washes over me, and I grit my teeth almost to the point that I swear they would crack and break.

Joel was right when he had said the pain was unbearable.

"You're awake," Dad states softly as he notices my open eyes. "It hurts, doesn't it?"

I nod, still gritting my teeth together.

"Tell my mom and sister that I'm sorry." I pant out as the pain overcomes me.

"You can tell them yourself when you heal, okay," Michael replies softly as he moves closer to my side.

"Just let me go. Marcus doesn't want me. If he did, he would have heard me scream for him. He doesn't care, and I don't want this life anymore, Dad." I argue with him.

"He will come back to you, Piper. Just hang on a little longer for me, please." He pleads.

"I'm not making any promises." I grit out just before I pass out again from the pain.

Could you really blame me for just wanting to give up? My life was going to be forever hiding and forever in danger.

Every day and every moment that I was alive would be lived looking over my shoulder.

Chapter Eleven

"She's been screaming in her sleep for hours now, Michael. What can we do to make this better?" Mom asks frantically.

"We need to find Marcus." He growls out in frustration again.

"Can I try something?" Mason's voice rings out in the distance.

My parents must answer him wordlessly because I soon feel his hand slip into mine.

Opening my eyes, I give him a weak smile while gritting my teeth together, the constant pain I was in, never letting up for even a single moment. I could feel every bone mending itself, and every so often, Michael would have to re-break a bone so that it could heal properly.

"Hey, Sweetheart, I'm going to try something if you're up for it." He whispers while caressing my cheek with his knuckles.

I lean into his touch, causing him to smile widely.

Looking back at my parents, he leans closer to me. So close that his lips brush against my ear as his breath warms my neck.

"I want you to take as much of my blood as possible. I want you to take as much as you need to heal." He suggests.

I shake my head.

"I will kill you if I do that." I grit out as quietly as possible.

"I don't care, as long as you're not in any more pain. Seeing you like this is tearing me up inside." He sighs roughly as he again caresses my cheek. "I love you, Piper, and I will do anything for you."

Shaking my head roughly, I refuse. I didn't want to hurt him, and I knew if I were to do what he wanted, I would surely kill him.

As he glances back at my parents talking in the corner of my room, I watch his face become determined. He wasn't going to give me much choice in this. I could see it clearly in his eyes.

He was willing to die for me.

In one fast move, he cuts his wrist and then forces it into my mouth. I fight against him, but my body quickly gives in as the blood flows over my tongue.

My fangs descend, and I bite into his wrist viciously.

"Mason, no," Michael yells out as he rushes over to us.

He has no choice but to stop when Mason's black wings unfold, shielding us both.

"Mason, let me pass. She will kill you." Michael growls as he continues to fight against Mason.

"I don't care, Michael. I can't see her like this anymore." Mason argues as he takes the force of my father's attack.

"She's not going to forgive you for this, Mason." My father stresses.

I watch in horror as Mason falls to his knees, pale and weak, but I can't stop myself.

My mind wars with itself. There was a part of me caring that I was killing him, while the other part didn't care one bit about what happened to him. It only craved more of his blood.

Suddenly, his arm is ripped away from my mouth.

I stare up in shock to see Marcus, his deep red wings wide as he pants while looking down at me with his equally deep red eyes.

"What happened, Piper?" He questions while he moves closer.

"She tried killing herself because of us," Mason answers from his place on the floor.

"Marcus, she needs your blood in order to heal faster," Dad stresses while helping Mason stand to his feet.

Marcus nods for a moment, but I see a bit of panic in his eyes as he watches me.

"Leave us, please." He demands.

Everyone nods before making quick exits.

Shutting the door, he leans his head against it and takes deep breaths. His wings fold away as his breathing slows, and he turns to face me.

I sit up slightly, feeling better from having Mason's blood flowing through my system. I could still feel my bones moving and healing, though.

It was an odd sensation, like sharp pins and then tingling mixed with a ton of itchiness.

"What's wrong, Marcus?" I ask, growing concerned by the look in his eyes.

"Nothing is wrong, Piper." He denies it while moving to my side.

Kneeling, he holds out his wrist for me.

"Tell me what it is that's wrong first, Marcus. I know something is wrong." I argue.

With a deep sigh, he rubs his hands roughly over his face.

"Just take my blood and heal first, then I'll tell you everything." He promises.

I nod, giving in.

"Tell me at least why you left me at school while I drink, okay." I insist, and he nods as he holds out his wrist once again.

I bite into him, and he grins while closing his eyes.

"I was stupid to leave, but I couldn't stand seeing you with him." He sighs before reopening his eyes. "I know I shouldn't have done what I did either; I know it upset you. I blame myself for everything that happened, Piper, and I'm sorry."

His other hand cups my cheek as I continue to take his blood in slowly.

"Please, forgive me for my actions." He pleads while looking deep into my eyes. "I heard you yell for me. I wanted to come to you so badly, but I couldn't. God, it killed me to know I couldn't help you."

"Why couldn't you come?" I ask before I lick his wounds closed and wipe my mouth with the back of my hand.

"That's what I need to tell you," Marcus growls as he stands. "I have some very dangerous angels after me. When I exposed myself, I became a target. There are many others out there that want me for my abilities."

"We can protect you, Marcus," I state, knowing that my father and Gabriel wouldn't allow any harm to come to him.

"No, Piper, I have to protect you. They have no idea what you are yet, and I'd like to keep it that way." He replies sternly.

"You're not leaving me again, Marcus." I bite out.

"Please, don't leave me." I then plead, seeing the resignation in his eyes.

"I have to leave until they lose interest in me again. Believe me; this is the last thing I want to do, but I must, I have to, in order to keep you safe." He replies.

"I'll run with you then." I try to compromise.

"You would really do that for me, Piper? You barely even know me." He questions.

I think for a moment. Would I leave with him? My mind once again warred with itself. I think about how much I had come to care for him, just like I had with Mason.

Of course, there was still a bit of hatred mixed in there for breaking my heart before, but I still cared enough.

"Of course I would, Marcus. I care about you." I reply and then sigh. "Anyway, won't it hurt you to be away from me?"

He nods while looking away from me. "Yes, it will hurt, but I can handle it for a while."

It was a lie.

"Stop trying to lie to me, Marcus," I snap as I stand.

He rushes over just as my legs give out.

Even though I was almost fully healed, I was extremely weak.

"Is there anything I can do to make it so you won't be in pain?" I question while he gently lies me back down on my bed.

Hovering over me, he smiles mischievously. "There is one way, but you're nowhere near ready for that, especially with me."

I open my mouth to respond, but he places his finger over my lips, stopping me. "I want that, but I won't push you into it. When it's right, it will happen, but until then, can you do me a favor?"

"Yes," I answer softly.

He sighs while closing his eyes. "Let yourself fall in love with Mason. I know he already loves you. Hell, he was willing to let you kill him. I need you to be with him so that he can keep you safe. He will treat you right."

"What about how I feel about you, Marcus? I can't just forget about the connection we have. I know there's something there. I can feel it." I argue lightly.

"You will forget all about me, Piper." He replies cryptically before continuing. "Maybe we'll have a chance when I return, but until then, let Mason have your heart." He whispers before kissing my lips.

Pulling back, his eyes blaze a fiery red as he stares deep into my eyes.

I could almost feel him in my mind sifting through my memories, and little by little, I felt him pulling every memory and thought about him from my mind.

When he finishes, he quickly stands to his feet.

My eyes close for a few moments before I reopen them to see a stranger standing in my room.

"Who the hell are you, and why are you in my room?" I cry out while backing away from him in fear on my bed.

The stranger smiles sadly before vanishing before my very eyes.

Mason and my father rush into the room, and I quickly stand to my feet before wrapping my arms around Mason's waist.

"What's wrong, Piper?" He asks while wrapping his arms around me.

"There was a stranger in my room." I pant out while scanning the room, expecting him to reappear.

"Wait, the only other person who was in here was Marcus. Where did he go?" Dad questions curiously.

"Who's Marcus?" I ask in frustration.

They quickly turn their attention back to me, wide-eyed.

"What is it? Why are you looking at me like that?" I question in confusion.

"Sweetheart, can you come here for a moment?" Dad asks.

I nod before slowly letting my arms fall from my grip on Mason.

Stepping in front of my father, he grabs my chin, forcing me to look directly into his dark eyes.

After a few moments, he curses out loudly.

Gabriel appears, and I yelp as I rush to hide behind Mason, thinking the stranger is returning.

Mason lets out a low chuckle as he pulls me back around to his front ánd wraps his arms around me protectively.

Gabriel glances around the room before looking towards Michael, who is still cursing to himself.

"What's going on, and why is your daughter suddenly afraid of me appearing?" Gabriel questions, stopping Michael's silent cursing.

"Well, to start, Marcus is gone. He must have gone back into hiding. Second, he took all of Piper's memories of him, and then he disappeared in front of her. That's why she's afraid of your sudden appearance, Gabriel. She's afraid he will return." Michael explains.

"He took her memories? Are you certain?" Gabriel asks, and my father nods. "If he did all of that, then there must be some sort of danger present. I don't think he would have done that for any other reason."

"If he could take her memories, what else could he have done?" Mason chimes in.

"He could be capable of anything, son. He's a very old and powerful angel." Gabriel answers softly.

We all stand in silence with everyone's eyes on me, as if they could physically see what that stranger had done to me.

I didn't feel any different. Well, that wasn't entirely true.

Something was missing.

"Piper, spread your wings for us for a moment, would you?" Michael requests.

I nod before looking up at Mason.

"Can you rip my shirt so they can come out?" I inquire with a slight grin.

He nods before twirling his finger for me to turn my back to him. He quickly rips two spots for my wings to expand.

As my wings unfold, Gabriel, Mason, and my father all gasp and then curse.

"What, what's wrong?" I question in fear.

"They're black, just like mine." Mason answers.

I laugh. "Why would they be any other color? They've always been black. You guys need to stop freaking out."

I glance between each of the men curiously as they watch me with frowns.

Michael turns his attention to Gabriel. "We have things we need to discuss." He states, and Gabriel nods while still watching me.

"Yes, we do." He agrees. "Mason, can you take care of Piper? She still needs to rest."

Mason nods, and they watch each other for a few moments, almost as if having a silent conversation. Mason nods once more before Gabriel and Michael leave the room.

"What was that all about?" I question.

He releases a huff of air as his hands glide over my wings. I sigh happily and close my eyes, enjoying his touch.

"How are you feeling?" He asks, avoiding my question.

I will my wings away and turn to face him.

Placing my hands on his chest, I look at his pale face, remembering how much blood I had taken from him.

I had nearly killed him.

"I should be asking you that. You saved me," I reply before biting my wrist and then holding it to his mouth. "Just take a little. I'm feeling much better, and my blood will help you heal faster."

He nods before pressing my wrist against his lips.

A few moments later, he pulls my wrist away, and I lick the wound closed.

Pulling me closer, he leans in and kisses me hard. His lips move roughly against mine as if he couldn't get enough.

I laugh softly as he pulls away. "What was that for?"

"I've wanted to do that since I watched you kiss Joel at school. I know that's horrible to say, but I was ticked that he was kissing you and not me, and I was ticked that you had chosen Marcus." He answers bashfully while rubbing his hand on the back of his neck.

"I didn't choose anyone else. I'm yours, Mason, forever yours." I answer softly before leaning up to kiss his lips.

"Are you sure about that?" He questions.

I nod and gaze deep into his eyes. "Of course, why wouldn't I be? You're the only one I care about, Mason."

"That's not exactly true." He mutters while looking away from me for a moment.

"What was that?" I push.

He shakes his head and looks back at me with a growing grin. "It was nothing, Sweetheart."

Taking my hand in his, he pulls me over to my bed. "Let's get some sleep, Piper. Both of us still need to heal."

I nod in agreement before lying down. I grin happily when he lies down behind me before pulling my body flush against his.

Being with him like this felt right, but at the same time, it felt as if something significant was missing.

Chapter Twelve

"**H**ow could he do that?" Mason whispers to someone in the room.

"We don't have a clue what he's capable of, Mason, but he must think that you can keep her safe," Gabriel answers softly.

I stay still, wanting to hear their conversation, which was obviously about me.

"This has gotten so messed up. I wanted her, but not like this, not when I know the second her memories come back that she will hate me for lying to her." Mason growls.

"Then don't lie to her, son. Tell her how you truly feel, and don't hold anything back." Gabriel replies.

"What do I say about Marcus?" Mason inquires.

Gabriel sighs. "You don't say anything, Mason. He took her memories of him away for a reason. It was probably to protect her, so we must take care in what we say."

"What about her wings? Are they going to be like that forever?" Mason whispers. "And for that matter, what about her thirst? What do we do about that?"

"We take one thing at a time. When it comes up, we will take care of it. She's in the best hands with all of us around her." Gabriel replies easily.

"Do we even know what kind of danger we're in?" Mason then asks, changing the subject.

"No, but we must keep alert. When you, Joel, and Cam go out tonight, I want all eyes on her. You must protect her at all costs." Gabriel commands.

"You know I will, Father," Mason replies confidently.

I listen as footsteps walk out of the room. The door shuts, and I stretch my arms over my head, pretending to just be waking up.

The bed dips with heavy weight as someone sits down on the edge.

"Feeling better?" Mason asks with a smile as I uncover my face.

Grinning, I nod. "Yes, I'm feeling much better."

"Do you think you're up for going out to the club, then?" He questions.

I nod. "I could use a night of dancing," I state, and then yelp when Gabriel appears out of thin air before us.

"I've got terrible news, Mason. We've been called to a council meeting." He announces.

"What? Now? We can't leave her like this," Mason growls while standing up.

"What's a council meeting?" I chime in curiously.

"It's a meeting of all the pure angels like your father and me. We also have to bring our eldest son with us," Gabriel answers.

"I won't leave her, Father," Mason growls out in anger.

"I know you don't want to, Mason, but we can't avoid it. We have to go. Joel can watch over her, and I'm almost certain that Marcus isn't far away." Gabriel replies.

They continue as if I'm not in the room.

"So, we just leave her with only Joel? That's not a very good idea, not when there's possible danger present." Mason argues.

Gabriel nods in agreement. "I know it's not ideal, but Marcus did hide her identity. She will be safe, Son."

"Again, who is this Marcus guy that you all keep talking about?" I clip out while standing on my feet, cutting into their conversation.

I wanted to know who this person was and why everyone kept bringing him up.

"He's no one important." Gabriel lies.

"I know you're lying, Gabriel, but you must have your reasons. I will find out who he is, though. You can count on it." I declare.

Both men stare at me for a few moments before chuckling.

Just then, my father and Cam come rushing into my room.

"I take it you two just heard of the meeting?" Gabriel snorts.

"Yes. This couldn't have happened at a worse time. Do you think they have any clue about her?" Dad questions frantically.

"I hope not, but we need to go. If they know anything, then they'll say something at the meeting." Gabriel answers.

Cam wraps his arm around me and pulls me close. "Don't worry about a thing, Sis. We'll be back before you know it." He whispers.

"I don't even know why I should even be worried. I don't understand any of this." I answer, frustrated.

"It's complicated, Piper, but the guy, Marcus, we keep talking about, he's dangerous, and he has taken an interest in you, which puts you in danger. Does that help you make more sense of why we're worried?" Mason answers, finally telling me part of the missing story.

I knew there was more to it, but I don't push for it, not right now.

I nod. "Yes, that explains it better, and at least now I know what to be worried about."

"Don't worry too much. Like Cam said, we'll be back before you know it." Mason assures while pulling me from Cam's embrace to hug me tightly against his body.

Laying my head on his chest, I listen closely to his heartbeat, which was beating frantically. He was scared, and that places a deeper fear in me.

"We better go before they grow suspicious of us." Gabriel sighs while watching Mason and me.

Pulling away, I look into Mason's eyes. "Just come back to me."

"I will, I promise." He answers before pressing a kiss to my forehead.

He steps back, and I watch as Gabriel smiles softly while placing his hands on Mason's shoulders. They disappear within seconds, and I'm left staring at an empty space.

"Be safe, Piper, and your mother will still be here for you if you need anything." Michael states before he and Cam disappear next.

I'm left alone in my room. I stand still for a moment, not knowing what to do. Without Mason with me, I felt lost.

Thankfully Joel walks in wearing a mischievous smirk.

"Looks like it's just going to be you and me, so what do you say to having a bit of fun?" He asks with a growing grin.

"I don't know, Joel. Is that even a good idea?" I stall while trying to hide my own growing grin.

"Yeah, you're right. A night of making others jealous and dancing doesn't sound like that much fun anyway." He sighs dramatically while looking down at his feet to hide his grin. "On the other hand, staying in and playing twister on your bed sounds better."

I smack him playfully as he grabs hold of me and then dumps me back onto my bed.

"Okay, okay, let's go out." I laugh as he tickles me.

"Good, you've got ten minutes to get into something sexy. Meet me downstairs; otherwise, I will come back and drag you out naked if I have to." He threatens with a laugh.

I push him away, and he quickly exits the room, shutting the door behind him.

"What am I even going to wear?" I mumble to myself.

After spending five minutes searching through my closet, I finally decide on a little blue halter-top dress.

Just as I'm trying to tie the back, Joel bursts through the door. I laugh when his face falls in mock disappointment.

"Can you help me tie this?" I question.

In an instant, his frown quickly changes back to a mischievous grin.

I turn my back to him as he moves closer.

As his hands lightly brush my skin, I'm taken back to the moments when we had been much closer, when we had both succumbed to my hormones.

Luckily, I was able to keep them under control now.

"I never regretted those moments with you, Piper," Joel states as if reading my mind.

"I never did either. I just wish what we had wouldn't have been influenced by other things." I reply before turning around to face him. "I really did fall hard for you. It killed me to hurt you like I did."

"It's all in the past now, and I'm not about to get in the way of my brother. He really does love you, you know. He did from the moment he saw you, and that's why I went after you first. Mason has always gotten everything he wants. I, on the other hand, get looked over, so I've become very competitive when it comes to certain things." He confesses.

"How about we start over as just really good friends?" I reply.

"Really good friends...." He laughs while trailing off as his lips form a cocky smirk. "...That knows what the other tastes like."

"Stop it." I snort and slap him playfully before moving to get my black knee-high boots.

"Why do you think everyone was called to that meeting, Joel?" I question while sitting on the edge of my bed to tug on the boots.

He stares out my window for a few moments before answering my lingering question. "I'm not sure, it doesn't happen often, but when it does, it's usually over something significant."

"How long do you think they will be away for?" I ask next.

"It could be hours, days, or even weeks." He answers honestly. "Let's keep busy so it won't seem so bad, okay."

I nod while standing to my feet. "Sounds like a plan."

Taking my hand in his, Joel leads me out of my room. Hannah coincidentally comes out of her room at the same time.

As her eyes meet Joel's, she blushes while he rubs the back of his neck bashfully.

"Are you two going out?" She asks, and I nod. "Is there any chance I can come along with you guys?"

"I don't think that's…." I begin.

"I think it's a great idea." Joel cuts me off, and I glare at him as he shrugs. "Go get ready, and we'll wait."

She rushes back into her room to dress, and I turn my full attention to Joel.

"You do realize we're now putting her in danger?" I clip out as I smack his chest.

"Yes, but she's human. She'll be fine, I promise. Anyway, it's best to have an extra set of eyes looking out for us." He explains.

"And you like her, don't you?" I question with a look.

He glances away, giving me my answer.

I groan loudly. "You're probably old enough to be her great, great grandfather. That's gross." I laugh at his mock look of hurt.

"I'll have you know that I'm younger than that. I'm only nineteen." He grins smugly. "Last I checked, you're with someone twice that. So, who's the gross one now?"

"Your brother, that's who; he's a gross old man," I answer, causing him to laugh abruptly.

"Well, you've been kissing that dirty old man." He snorts and then quiets quickly when my sister walks back out dressed similarly to me but in deep brown with matching boots.

"I'm all ready when you two are." She mumbles softly.

I elbow Joel when he doesn't take his eyes off of her.

He coughs and then holds out his arm to her. She takes it, and they take off down the stairs together, making me the third wheel.

This night was going to be a drag.

I sigh and roll my eyes as I move to follow them.

I was not only going to worry about the danger I was in, but now I had to worry about my little sister, who shouldn't even be going out with us.

Heck, she shouldn't have even been going to a club.

As we head to the front door, Mom stops us. My last hope was for Mom to say no.

"Have fun, kids, and watch out for Hannah, you two." She commands while pointing to Joel and me, squashing my hopes of my sister having to stay behind where it was safe.

"I'll watch out for them both, Helen," Joel reassures her.

She nods while watching us as we leave the house.

Sliding into the cab of Joel's truck, I inwardly groan. Joel and Hannah were barely millimeters away from each other. They were so close that she may as well have been sitting on his lap.

I wasn't going to have to watch out for danger tonight; I was going to have to watch out for these two and make sure they didn't do anything stupid together.

****

As we drive past the long line for the club, I grin.

"How are we ever going to get in? That's a really long line." Hannah questions, sounding defeated.

"Don't worry about that; I know the head bouncer," I reply confidently when I spot Duke standing by the entrance.

I knew that with another friendly smile, a touch, and a small promise that he would let us all in without a problem.

We get out of Joel's truck and meet up at the front.

I loop my arm through Joel's, and Hannah does the same before we walk toward the front of the line together.

"This is such a rush. Can you feel it, Joel?" I grin as everyones' jealousy floats around me.

"No, I can't. I'm not like you, Piper. I'm a light angel like my father." He answers.

I pause to look at him oddly.

"How did I not know that?" I mutter.

"You've never really seen my wings out, that's why." He replies with a wink as we approach Duke.

"Well, aren't you a sight for sore eyes, Miss Piper." Duke greets as he looks around us before looking back at me curiously. "Where's Cameron?"

"He had a meeting to attend, so it's just going to be me, my sister, and her boyfriend, Joel," I explain as I move closer. "Cam wanted me to have fun tonight, and since he isn't with me, maybe you could dance with me when you get a break?"

"I definitely will. Go ahead in, and I'll see you soon, Sweetheart." He replies.

I kiss his cheek and bounce back to Joel's side.

Looping my arm back through his, I lead him and my sister into the club.

Hannah stops to kiss Duke on his other cheek before she catches up with us. She definitely knew how to flirt.

Duke's grin turns smug as the other bouncer eyes him up.

Walking into the club, I quickly get separated from Joel and my sister. I look around for them even though it's useless.

The place was crowded.

Giving up, I decide to head over to the bar. They would see me there if they were looking, which I doubted they were.

Sitting down at a seat at the bar, the bartender winks at me while serving another person.

"Where's Cam at tonight?" He questions while making his way over to me.

"He's not here; it's just me tonight," I answer.

"You won't be alone for long then." He grins before placing a drink in front of me. "It's the same as last time, and don't worry about paying. I'll put it on Cam's tab." He assures before he turns to leave.

He pauses before turning back around. "If you need anything, just yell for me. My name is J.D. Cam would kick my ass if anything happened to you, Piper."

"Thanks, J.D.; just keep the drinks coming, okay," I reply while drinking the one in front of me as he laughs out with a nod.

After three songs and about six drinks, I finally spot my sister and Joel coming my way.

"Where have you two been?" I question a bit harshly as they come to stand beside me.

"We were just dancing," Hannah answers as she sits in the seat next to me.

J.D. comes over, and I point to her. "Only water for her. She's my sister and underage."

He grins and walks away before returning with a glass of water for her.

"Can I get any more for you?" He asks.

"Not right now. I'm going to take my turn dancing, but have one ready for me when I get back." I reply and then turn towards Joel for a moment before turning back to J.D.

He nods as he grins.

"None for him either, I get it." He laughs while looking at my sister and Joel.

"Thanks, J.D." I laugh as I stand and allow Joel to sit. "I'll be right back, okay?"

He nods while looking directly at my sister.

Growling, I grab his chin roughly to make him actually notice me.

"I will kick your ass if you even touch her, Joel," I warn, and he nods as his eyes widen.

I back away into the crowd as he watches. I motion between him and my eyes and visibly see him gulp before he turns back towards the bar.

I grin to myself as I turn and head in the direction of the restrooms.

While there, I cringe when I hear two men enter.

"Did you see that girl in blue at the bar?" One asks, and I roll my eyes.

"Yeah, but J.D. said she was off-limits." The other man answers as he turns on the water.

"I don't care what J.D. says. When we go back out there, I'm going after her." The first one states.

I lift my nose in the air as I get a strong scent of blood. The craving for it takes over me, and my fangs bite down into my bottom lip.

The hunger taking over completely makes me do what I do next.

"If that's the way you're going to be, then it's game on, brother. I wonder what her…." He trails off as I exit the stall that I had been hiding in.

"Don't let me stop you from what you were saying." I insist while going to the sink to wash my hands.

They stand in place, watching my every move.

Both men had dark brown short-cut hair, and their faces were chiseled much the same, but those were the only things they had in common.

One had light blue eyes, while the other had hazel. Both men were built sturdy from what I could see, even though one was about a foot shorter than the other.

I could also sense that both were angels, and that simple fact only makes my thirst for their blood even stronger.

I glance between the men and grin as I notice their eyes dilate.

Thanks to my pheromones, neither of them would know what I was about to do.

Gabriel had explained how they helped me to take blood unnoticed and how the angel who had been fed upon would never know what had happened.

If I did things right, they would only think I had kissed them.

Turning to the taller one who I had interrupted, I smile. "Please, finish what you were about to say."

"I was just wondering what you must taste like." He answers softly while tilting his head to look at me curiously.

"That's funny because I was just thinking that about you too." I flirt while stepping closer to him.

Shaking his head hard, his eyes narrow in on me as he fights against the pheromones that my body is releasing.

I step forward, hoping to get him back under my control, but it doesn't work.

His eyes flash into two pools of black as he lifts my chin. "What are you, Darling?" He asks softly as he searches my eyes.

I step back in alarm, only to bump into the other guy standing directly behind me.

"Don't leave us yet, Sweetheart." He whispers into my ear as his hands grab onto my hips.

J.D. suddenly walks in with Duke, and I sigh with relief.

"Back away from her now, Alec. She's protected," J.D. commands.

"Why is she protected, J.D.?" The guy, Alec, in front of me, questions, refusing to back away from me.

"That's no concern of yours. Just get away from her." Duke growls as he steps forward.

He growls, which startles me, causing me to press back against the guy behind me. His arms wrap around me as I watch J.D.'s and Duke's faces change.

They must be the wolves Cam had mentioned before.

I wished now that I had asked him more about them. That knowledge would have come in handy right about now.

Throwing his hands into the air, Alec surrenders. "Fine, I give up. It's not worth getting into a fight with your pack, J.D. Come on, Sid. We need to leave now."

It takes a few moments for Sid to let me go, but he finally does. I watch as they both exit the restroom quickly.

Duke goes over to the door and locks it quickly before turning back to me.

The hunger I had felt overcomes me again, and I growl at them both, showing my fangs as my wings unfold.

"Holy…" J.D. whispers as he backs away next to Duke. "No one ever told me she had fangs."

In a flash, the stranger from my room appears in front of me.

I don't think for a moment. I go in for the attack, his blood causing my mind to go blank with need.

He chuckles softly as my fangs sink into his skin. His hands hold me tightly to him, making me feel whole again. That missing piece is suddenly gone.

"What are you doing here, Marcus?" J.D. questions curiously.

"I had to come. I had to take care of my girl here." Marcus sighs.

"Why does she have fangs and wings? I didn't think your kind came in female form." Duke stresses.

"She's one of a kind, and you must keep her a secret. She's just like me." He confesses.

"That would have been a nice thing to warn us about, Marcus. Especially considering she almost exposed herself to two other angels." J.D. growls out.

Marcus curses, and I pull away after closing his wounds.

I sigh in contentment and lean my head against his chest.

"Can I ask you and your pack a huge favor, J.D.?" Marcus asks softly.

J.D. must nod because Marcus continues. "Can you watch over her until Michael and Cam return? If there are other angels around, then she may be in danger, and that young angel, Joel, isn't going to be enough to protect her."

"We will watch her for you, only as long as my pack has your protection as well," J.D. states calmly.

"Of course, I wouldn't leave you and your pack unprotected." Marcus agrees as he gently rubs his hand over my hair. "One last thing. I have been taking her memories so she won't remember any of this, not me, not this conversation, and not those others. I have to do this in order to keep her safe, so watch what is said around her, okay?"

"Okay, Marcus, you know we will do anything you ask. Plus, I've grown to have a soft spot for this little girlie." Duke answers with a light laugh.

Lifting my chin, Marcus looks directly into my eyes.

"Please, don't take them away. I don't want to feel the emptiness again." I plead.

His eyes soften, and he strokes his fingers across my cheek before his eyes flash red.

A moment later, I fade into the darkness.

Chapter Thirteen

Getting ready for school the next morning, I groan while slipping on a comfortable pair of flip-flops.

My head was killing me, and with every move, I made it only hurt worse.

"How are you feeling today, Piper?" Hannah asks as she walks in with a glass of water and a plate stacked with toast.

"I feel terrible. I can't even remember what happened." I state while taking the water from her hand and drinking a sip.

My stomach felt well compared to my head, which I thought was odd, considering alcohol was supposed to make you feel sick to your stomach the next day.

"J.D. told us that he found you passed out in the men's restroom. He told us that you had had a lot to drink, too, which is probably why you can't remember anything, and why you're feeling terrible today." Hannah explains while holding out the toast for me to take.

Munching on a piece, I sigh, not feeling at all hungry.

Thinking back, I hadn't eaten in days, and I wonder for a moment what that could be all about. It was something that I would have to find out from Joel.

Maybe it was an angel thing.

"Did you have fun last night?" I ask, changing the subject.

I wanted to know just what she had gotten up to.

"Yes, I had an amazing time with Joel." She gushes.

"You like him, don't you?" I question with my brow raised.

"I do, I really do, and I know what you're thinking, Piper, but I could care less that he's an angel. It just makes him that much more irresistible." She states seriously.

"And what will you do when he has to leave you?" I question, wanting her to fully understand that whatever was between them would never last.

"I will go with him." She answers simply.

Knowing that I had nothing that would turn her away from him, I give up. I didn't want to fight with her. So, I was giving in for now, but I would be talking to Joel later so he could talk some sense into her.

"Fine, just promise me that you'll be careful. Being with someone takes a lot of work, and it's not always the first one you fall for that will be the one who's meant for you." I answer softly.

"Thanks, Piper. I promise I'll be careful." She smiles sweetly. "Now, are you ready for school? Joel's taking us since you're not feeling good."

I nod before getting off my bed and standing to my feet.

I rub at my temples as they begin to throb.

Maybe school wasn't the best idea, but lying in bed all day wondering when Cam, Michael, Mason, and Gabriel were coming back would be worse.

"I'm ready, I think." I breathe out.

I was already dressed in a pair of jeans and a white top. All I needed to do was slip on a pair of shoes to match.

Once I slip my shoes on, I follow Hannah out of the house, although a bit slower than usual.

Getting into the truck, I slide over next to Joel, and Hannah sits next to me before she slams her door shut.

I grab my head and groan.

"That's the worst sound in the world." I moan before laying my head forward against the dash of the truck.

"Should you even be going to school like this, Piper?" Joel questions just before he slams his door shut.

"Are you trying to make my head explode?" I growl out while turning my head to glare at him.

"Sorry, Piper, I didn't think." He chuckles and raises his hands in surrender.

"Let's just get to school so I can get this day over with and maybe feel a little better." I groan once more.

"Okay, close your eyes on the way. Hopefully, that will help a little bit." Joel suggests as he starts the truck and begins our trip.

I nod and lay my head on his shoulder before closing my eyes.

"I hope Mason and Cam come back soon," Hannah whispers.

"I hope so, too; I'm really worried about her," Joel replies.

The rest of the ride is quiet, and I thankfully nod off to sleep.

"Piper, we're here," Joel announces as he shakes me awake only a few minutes later.

I groan. "That was too fast."

"Yeah, I know, I even took the long way to give you more time, but if we don't go in soon, we're going to be late," Joel explains.

I groan more as I look around the parking lot filled with cars but absent of the students that generally lingered outside.

I also notice that my sister was nowhere to be seen either.

"Where's my sister?" I ask.

"She already went inside. She wanted you to have just a bit more rest." He answers.

I nod and then scoot across the seat to get out of the passenger side of the truck. Once the fresh air hits my face, I take a deep breath and feel better, if only for a moment.

"Are you going to be alright, Piper?" Joel asks while coming around to my side of the truck.

I nod. "I'll be fine. I've just got to get past this horrible headache. I really shouldn't have drunk so much last night."

"Well then, let's get you inside the school." He breathes out before wrapping his arm around my waist to help me stand.

"Thanks, Joel," I whisper as he guides me into the school.

Once at my locker, he lets me free with a look of concern.

"I'll be fine," I reassure him.

He nods once, not looking at all like he believes me, before he turns around to leave.

I watch his back disappears around the corner before returning to my locker.

"There you are, Darling." A voice rings out behind me.

I turn around to face a tall guy with brown hair that I had never seen before. A soft groan falls from my lips as I place my hand on my head and close my eyes.

"I have no idea who you are, but please tell me we didn't do anything stupid last night. Actually, scratch that, don't tell me. I'd rather not know." I answer before opening my eyes to look into his light blue eyes.

He scrunches his face in confusion. "Wait, are you trying to tell me that you don't remember anything from last night?"

"Nope, I don't remember a thing. My friends and the bartender told me that I had way too much to drink and passed out in the men's restroom." I reply.

"Oh, well, since you don't remember, I'll just play this off as if this is the first time we've met." He laughs as he holds out his hand.

I take it in mine and smile.

"I'm Alec, and you are?" He questions as his hand squeezes mine gently.

"I'm Piper," I answer.

He leans in closer, grinning wickedly.

"I love the name, and just to ease your pretty little heart, we didn't do anything other than talk last night." He states before pulling back as his grin turns smug. "I did almost get a kiss, though."

"Be glad you didn't because my boyfriend would have kicked your butt if you did." I laugh as I turn to get my books and shut my locker door.

The bell rings out suddenly, causing me to drop everything in my hands as I grab hold of my head.

"Whoa, are you okay?" Alec questions as the bell thankfully stops ringing.

"Yeah, I've just got the worst headache you can possibly get, but I'll be fine," I answer as we bend down to pick up my books.

"This is probably the last place you need to be if it hurts that bad." He argues lightly as he snatches my books from my hands and then stands to his feet before holding his other hand out to me.

"You're not the first person to say that, and I think that maybe you're right, but I don't have a way to get home, so I might as well just get through the day," I reply as I take his hand and allow him to pull me to my feet.

"Since you're so determined, at least let me walk you to your first class." He laughs softly.

I nod as I thread my arm through his. We walk silently together down the hallway and towards my classroom.

"Thanks, Alec," I whisper as we reach the door to my first-period class.

"Anytime, Piper, just yell if you need me." He replies before waving as he walks away.

Chapter Fourteen

Somehow, I manage to make it through half of the day and into the lunchroom, where I finally collapse in my seat next to Beth.

"What happened to you, Piper? You look like death." She whispers.

"I feel like death." I groan.

"You look worse than you did this morning, Piper. Are you sure you shouldn't just go home?" Joel asks as he sits across from me.

"I don't know, Joel. I probably should go home, but I don't want to be there alone." I answer.

Everyone goes quiet for a moment before I glance up to see Alec and another guy sit down with us at our table.

I force a smile when Alec looks at me, concerned.

"You're really not looking good, Darling." He states.

"Who are you guys?" Joel clips out quickly.

"I'm Alec, and this is my brother Sid. We met Piper at the club last night." He answers Joel as he points to me, and I nod.

"He's really sweet, Joel, so leave them alone," I reply sternly.

He nods as his brow furrows and his mouth turns down into a frown.

Just past him, I spot Sara, Sasha, and Jayden heading our way.

I curse and lay my forehead on the cool table. "Can't they just stay away for one day? Would it kill them not to always hit on the new guys?"

"Hey, Piper, you look like crap today." Jayden laughs menacingly.

"Oh hey, Jayden, you look like crap today, too. It must be a new fashion thing, huh," I answer while picking my head up to glare at her.

"At least I look better than you. I see Mason and Marcus finally left you. Are these the replacements?" She replies smugly.

"Who the hell is Marcus? And no, Mason didn't leave me. He's just away for the day." I growl out and then point toward Alec and his brother. "As for these two, have at them if they want you."

She looks at me, confused for a moment, before looking around the table.

Her mouth opens and closes for a moment before she finally speaks. "You must be messed up if you don't know who Marcus, your boyfriend, is, or do you just go through men so fast that you can't remember their names."

"Enough, leave her alone now, you stupid bimbo. No one here cares for what you have to say, and I, for one, don't want to look at you for another second. You make me sick." Alec spits out at her, defending me.

Everyone in the whole lunchroom grows quiet hearing his words.

Sara and Sasha glance at each other and then at Jayden, who was standing there with her mouth open as if in shock that someone would find her repulsive.

"Leave, now," Sid growls out next. "I can't eat my lunch with you just standing there."

Stopping her foot in anger, we watch as Jayden's face turns bright red.

"Neither of you are good enough for me anyway." She sputters before she finally turns to rush out of the room.

I bark out in laughter and turn my attention to Sid and Alec.

"You two just made my day." I laugh as they both grin.

"That was totally harsh, but you've won me over for standing up to them." Joel laughs as he bumps fists with Sid.

Turning to me, he smiles sadly. "Mason should have done that last time; maybe he should take a page from these two's book."

"Yeah, he should have," I mumble, my laughter disappearing with the reminder.

"You're saying that this guy, Mason, your boyfriend, didn't turn that girl down?" Alec asks, looking angry.

"Yes, he let her sit on his lap while Piper sat there watching it all happen. He was a real jerk to her that day." Beth answers for me.

"Don't leave out the part where I tried to get back at him by kissing Joel," I add with a snort of laughter.

"Oh, that's good. You're a naughty one, aren't you?" Sid chuckles.

"You have no idea." Joel snorts while looking at me with a smirk.

"You seem to be full of surprises, Darling." Alec snorts before he joins in their laughter.

As I continue to laugh, I catch Sid from the corner of my eye-grabbing a knife off of the table before moving it under the table.

I try not to focus on him, but when the scent of his blood hits me, I'm forced to close my eyes and grind my teeth together.

I had to gain control of this, and fast.

I would expose my fangs to the world if I wasn't careful.

What was Sid trying to do anyway? He couldn't possibly know what I was, but I definitely knew what he was now.

There was no doubt in my mind that he was an angel, and I would guess that he was a dark one.

"Piper, are you still feeling sick?" Alec asks, breaking into my thoughts.

I open my eyes and turn to him.

His eyes widen before he smirks.

Leaning in his breath warms my neck. "I know what you are now, and if you need my blood, you can have it, Darling."

My eyes go wide as he pulls away.

"Piper, what's wrong?" Joel asks while looking between Alec and me.

"Nothing's wrong. I think I just need some fresh air." I answer while still looking at Alec.

"Do you want me to come out with you?" Joel asks.

I shake my head.

"I'll go with you, Piper. I need a smoke break anyway." Alec answers before standing to his feet.

He holds his hand out to me, and I reluctantly take it. We walk out of the lunchroom together and then down the hall.

When we reach a door, Alec quickly pulls me through it and into an empty supply room before locking the door behind him.

Facing me, he strokes my cheek with the back of his hand.

"It's been a long time since I've had the chance to be with a vampire." He admits shyly.

"How did you figure it out?" I question, playing it out.

It was best that he thought I was a vampire rather than an angel.

"I had an idea at the club, but with what my brother just did, it made it easy to figure out when your eyes flashed red." He replies as he leans closer to me while taking a deep breath. "Your scent is more powerful than any other vampire that I've ever encountered, though."

Cocking his head to the side, he studies me as he continues to talk. "What I don't understand is your taste in blood, you didn't once react to human blood, but the second you smelled our blood, you could barely control yourself."

"And what exactly are you?" I question, even though we both knew that I already knew.

"I'm a dark angel, as is my brother." He replies as his hands grip my hips.

"I know you're hungry, and I'm willing to allow you to taste me as long as I can taste you." He whispers before he searches my eyes.

My fangs bite into my bottom lip before I nod once.

He grins before his lips crash into mine.

His lips then quickly move from my mouth to my neck, caressing every inch.

He elicits a low moan from me, and his hands grip my hips tighter. "Your boyfriend was stupid to even leave you alone for a moment, Darling. If you were mine, I'd never leave your side."

"That's enough talking, Alec," I growl as I grab onto his head to angle his neck just right.

He grins widely as I go in for the bite, his hands holding me tightly against his body.

As my fangs sink in, spilling his blood, I jump up to wrap my legs around his waist. He wordlessly moves us so my back is against the wall.

He groans as I lap up his blood slowly, enjoying the taste.

After a few long moments, I remind myself to stop.

I pull back, making sure to lick his wound closed.

Still holding me against the wall, his lips crash onto mine once again before they trail down my neck while I close my eyes.

"You're not going to hurt me now that you know what I am, are you?" I pant.

"I would never hurt you. I'll keep your secret as long as I stay your dirty little secret." He replies with a sexy growl.

"What about when my boyfriend returns?" I question.

He pulls back to look into my eyes. "Does it really matter? I can tell that you must not be pleased with him, and from what you told me before about him not standing up to that girl for you, he doesn't deserve you."

"I do care for him, Alec, and I don't want to hurt him, not like this. But, if we do this more, then it won't involve any more than just me taking your blood. Is that okay?" I reply.

"That's fine, but I will have you eventually." He answers seriously.

I could tell that he wasn't going to give up trying to win me over, and I couldn't exactly say I wasn't happy about that because he was right. Something between Mason and I was missing.

"I know you won't." I smile sweetly as I kiss his lips gently once more before standing to my feet. "Since I just took blood from you, please don't tempt me again so soon. I don't want to end up hurting you, okay," I warn.

He nods in understanding. "I know how this all works, Darling, so don't worry about me." He answers before letting me go and then moving over to the door.

He unlocks it and peeks out before leaving me alone in the room.

Suddenly, a stranger appears with a flash of bright light in the room with me. He grabs hold of my arms, stopping me from running away.

"Don't be scared of me, Piper." He whispers.

I stop fighting him.

"Who are you?" I ask curiously as he pulls my body against his.

We fit together perfectly, like two puzzle pieces.

"I'm Marcus, Sweetheart." He sighs. "I shouldn't have left you. I'm sorry for that, but I didn't expect you to begin messing around with another dark angel. What are you doing, Sweetheart?" He rambles as I lean my head against his chest.

"I don't know what I'm doing," I confess. "I just want this emptiness to go away."

"I do too, and I'm working on getting back to you, but we will still have to be apart for a little while longer." He answers, causing me to break down into sobs.

"I don't even know who you are, but being here with you feels right." I cry as he wipes away my tears. "Are you the reason I've been forgetting things and getting headaches?"

"Yes, I am. I've been taking your memories of me away to keep you safe. It hasn't been working very well, though." He chuckles softly.

"Don't take them away this time. I want to remember you. I need to remember you." I plead as my hands travel across his chest.

"I have to, Sweetheart." He whispers in pain while closing his eyes.

"No, you don't," I argue.

"If I leave you with this memory, will you do something for me?" He asks.

I nod. "I will do anything."

He grins before he speaks. "Don't let anyone touch you like Alec just did. You belong to me and only me, okay."

I nod in agreement just before his lips touch mine.

His kiss was more passionate than I had ever felt and left my head spinning with happiness.

As he pulls away, his eyes flash red, and for a moment, I feel everything. I felt all of my memories of him return, and I smile.

"I love you, Marcus," I whisper.

His eyes flash a brighter red, and all those memories flood back out in a rush causing me to collapse in his arms.

"I love you too, Piper." Is the last thing I hear before I blackout.

Chapter Fifteen

Waking up still in the supply closet, I groan.

I was tired of having these blackouts and not remembering what had happened before them.

Touching my lips, I grin. I did remember being kissed by a stranger, but other than that, I couldn't remember much about him other than that he had made me feel complete.

"Piper, are you still in here?" Alec asks as he peeks through the door.

"Yes, I'm still here," I answer.

"Seriously, what happened?" He questions as he opens the door allowing the light to flood in. "You've been missing for a while."

"I blacked out right after you left. I just woke up." I explain while taking his outstretched hand to stand. "How long was I out?"

"It's the end of the school day." He answers while watching me curiously.

"And everyone is just now looking for me?" I question.

He shrugs. "I thought you just went home, but when Joel couldn't find you, I figured maybe you fell asleep in here or something."

"Well, I'm glad you knew where to look." I laugh softly.

"I will always be able to find you, Darling." He whispers.

"Why is that? Are you some sort of tracker?" I laugh jokingly.

"Actually, that's exactly what I am; I track down others. I'm a hunter of sorts." He answers seriously.

"Is that why you're here then, to track someone?" I question, needing to know how close he was to finding out my true identity or if any of my family or friends were in danger.

"Yes, I was sent here to track down two unique angels, but I haven't had any luck finding them so far." He sighs roughly before running his fingers through his hair.

"What does your brother do?" I inquire next curiously.

"I shouldn't be telling you anything, Piper. It's dangerous for you to know any of this." He answers as his hands grasp my hips.

"Just tell me. I need to know if I'm in any kind of danger." I plead while wrapping my arms around his neck.

"My brother is a very dangerous angel, and it would be best for you to stay on his good side. Where I track, he's the one who goes in and does the dirty work when I find what needs to be found." He explains quickly.

"You aren't in any danger, Darling. I wouldn't let anything happen to you." He promises with a light kiss.

"I trust you," I answer.

I trusted him and felt that he wouldn't intentionally put me in harm's way, but I needed to be on alert when I was around him. I had to warn everyone else about his brother, though. He could prove to be a massive problem if things went south.

He grins. "Good. Now, let's get you out of here and home where you can rest properly."

"Is everyone else here?" I ask as we walk out of the supply closet.

"No, everyone else went to look for you elsewhere. We're supposed to meet at your house when one of us finds you." He replies.

"I'm glad they aren't here. They worry about me too much since I've been having these blackouts." I sigh.

"Do you have any idea why they are happening?" He questions, and I shake my head.

"How old are you?" He then asks, stopping us in the middle of the hallway.

"I'm eighteen," I answer easily before realizing that I had completely forgotten my birthday somewhere along the line.

So much had happened in the last few days that that had been the last thing on my mind.

"Wait, your eighteen, or your death age was eighteen?" He questions while looking at me oddly.

"I'm only eighteen. This drinking blood stuff is all new to me." I answer honestly.

His brow scrunches for a moment. "Well, that explains the blackouts then, but it doesn't explain your taste for only angel blood."

"It's the only blood I've ever tasted. Would that be a good reason?" I ask.

He nods to himself. "Yeah, I guess that would explain it. I've had many vampires tell me that angel blood is better than any other and that they never want anything else once they taste it."

"It drives me absolutely crazy when I smell it. I practically lose complete control of myself." I reply as we begin moving again.

When we reach the parking lot, I smile widely, spotting Mason and Cam just getting out of Mason's truck.

"I take it that those are friends of yours?" Alec asks.

I nod before letting him go to run towards my brother and Mason.

Mason reaches me first and swings me around before pulling me in for a much-needed deep kiss.

He pulls back just as Alec walks closer.

I hold out my hand and smile brightly. "Mason, this is…."

"Alec. Why are you here?" Cam interrupts me.

"Ah, Cam, I see you're still mad at me," Alec replies as he glances between us for a moment.

Cam growls out, and Alec smirks.

"I should be asking you what you're doing here, Cam. Shouldn't you be off working with Michael?" Alec questions with a curious look.

"I'm here visiting Mason. Michael is here working too." Cam replies as he nods to Mason. "Why are you here, though? Is Sid here also?"

"Yes, he's here, and we're working, but you don't have to worry about anything. We're looking for something we have yet to find." Alec answers, skirting around everything we had just discussed.

"So, Piper, is this the boyfriend you've told me so much about?" Alec asks while turning his attention to me, thankfully changing the subject.

"Yes, this is him," I answer while wrapping my arms around Mason's waist.

Alec smirks at the sight but doesn't say another word.

I could only guess what he was thinking.

I, on the other hand, felt a boulder of guilt hanging heavily on my shoulders since I had been in the supply closet kissing Alec earlier. I had to be the worst girlfriend ever.

"You're a lucky guy, Mason. Piper is certainly one of a kind." Alec declares with a knowing smirk.

"Yes, I am," Mason replies while grinning down at me.

"Treat her right, or you'll lose her," Alec warns before he begins walking away.

We watch as he gets into a sleek black car before driving off.

I let out a sigh of relief until Cam and Mason look directly at me. I knew they wanted to know exactly what was going on.

I let out a loud, dramatic groan.

It was going to be a long ride home.

"I'll tell you everything on the way home, guys." I insist.

"That's all we want because this whole thing is as confusing as hell," Mason replies as he gestures around absently.

"Yeah, no kidding, we leave you for less than two days, and you've met the single most dangerous tracker in the angel world." Cam breathes out as he jumps into the truck behind me.

"Yeah, I know that, but he doesn't have a clue that I'm even an angel," I answer, causing Cam and Mason to look at me oddly.

"What does he think you are then?" Mason questions.

"He thinks I'm a vampire." I laugh softly.

Both men are quiet for a few moments before they burst into laughter.

"Seriously, he thinks you're a vampire?" Cam continues to laugh loudly as he grips his stomach.

"Yes, but only because I ended up biting him. I thought for sure that he would know instantly what I was." I reply as my laughter dies down.

"You bit him?" Mason stops laughing, and I nod. "Please, tell me you didn't do anything more than just bite him."

"I only bit him, Mason." I lie, hoping he wouldn't catch it.

He watches me for a second but then nods as he looks out the window. He probably didn't believe me, but now wasn't the time to discuss what I had done.

Cam's hand slips into mine as the truck starts, and we head down the road toward home. He gives me the tiniest of squeezes, filling me with comfort.

At least I knew I would always have my brother by my side no matter what happened.

Even though we hadn't known each other long, an unbreakable bond had formed between us.

"Did Alec say anything about what or who he was looking for?" Cam asks, breaking the silence.

"He just said that he and his brother were sent here to look for two unique angels. He also told me that his brother could be dangerous but that he would keep me safe from him." I answer quietly.

"Do you think you can trust him to keep you safe if he discovers your true identity?" Cam questions next.

I respond with a sarcastic laugh as I shake my head. "You know we can't trust anyone; no one can know that I'm a female angel."

"Do you think you can stay close enough to get more information out of him without putting yourself in any more danger?" Cam questions curiously.

"You're not seriously asking her that, are you, Cam?" Mason growls.

"Yes, I am. If we know what he's found, then we can stay one step ahead of him and his brother." Cam answers calmly.

"And what do we do if he finds out what Piper is? What do we do if he takes her away?" Mason bites out in anger as we pull into his driveway.

"That won't happen, Mason." I declare while placing my hand on his arm to calm him.

"You can't actually promise me that, Piper. You won't be able to keep yourself hidden forever if you're getting as close as I know you are." He disagrees.

I open my mouth to say something, but he quickly stops me. "You don't have to explain anything to me, Piper. I know we're nothing. I know you care about me and think you love me, but you don't. So please don't lie to me anymore. I, at least, want to know that I can trust you."

"I'm sorry, Mason, I really am, and I will be honest with you from now on. What happened between Alec and me was a mistake, and I'd like to blame my hunger for my actions, but I could have stopped myself from kissing him." I explain while bowing my head in shame.

"Just don't allow it to happen again." He whispers as he tugs my chin up to look into my eyes. "There's someone out there that does care what you do. He loves you more than I ever could."

"Will you forgive me, at least?" I plead.

"No, I can't, not yet, at least. You still hurt me, and it's going to take some time. I can't just forgive you so quickly." He answers before opening his door to exit the truck.

As it slams shut, I feel the door slam shut on the relationship that we could have had. It felt as if a knife had been slammed into my heart.

I never wanted to hurt anyone, but I was glad I had been honest with him.

"Everything will be alright, Piper. Just let him have some time to himself. He'll come back around." Cam promises.

"I hope you're right, Cam." I breathe out as we exit the truck.

"When are you going to learn, Sis? I'm always right." Cam teases as we walk across the grass to our front porch.

Laughing with him, I roll my eyes.

Walking into the house, I'm greeted by Mom, Hannah, Michael, and Gabriel.

"Where was she?" Michael asks Cam as if I'm not in the room.

"She passed out in a supply room at the school." He answers.

"Why were you there, Piper?" Michael questions curiously as he turns his attention toward me.

I sigh roughly. "It's honestly a long story, Dad, but I don't have any clue why I keep blacking out. This was the second time in two days that it's happened. Last night was the worst, and I had the worst headache when I woke up. This time I don't have a headache, thank goodness."

"Marcus, he's been seeing you for some reason, but why?" He mutters quietly to himself.

"Is that what his name is?" I ask softly, breaking his concentration.

His eyes glance at mine before looking at Cam.

"What do you mean?" He asks.

"There was a man. I remember him from before I blacked out at the school." I blush as I look down at my feet. "He kissed me, but that's all I can remember. I don't even really know what he looked like, everything in my mind is a blur, but I remember a man being there." I explain.

"So, wait, it wasn't just Alec that you kissed today?" Cam questions abruptly.

I turn to look at him.

I lower my eyes and nod. "I guess so. I didn't think about the other guy until Dad said his name."

"Wait, did you say Alec? As in, Alec, the hunter?" Gabriel questions this time, breaking into our conversation.

Both Cam and I nod before Gabriel and Michael curse.

"Before you two go and get mad at Piper, hear me out." Cam insists as he holds up his hands. "Alec is interested in Piper, but not for the reasons you're thinking. He thinks she's a vampire. He has no clue what she is."

"Is that true?" Michael asks, looking at me.

I nod.

"He has also talked to Piper about why he and his brother are here. He's giving her valuable information, so I told her to stay close to him. I figure that way, we can stay one step ahead of him." Cam adds.

"It's dangerous for Piper to be close to him, though. Do you think it's wise?" Gabriel questions with worry lacing his voice.

"Alec admitted today that he would protect me. I don't think he would harm me even if he did figure out my identity. He seems to be nothing like his brother." I voice.

"You don't know what they've done, Piper. He may seem like a trustworthy angel, but he has done some very unthinkable things to become the great hunter that he is now. He has never failed at doing a job." Gabriel explains.

He was trying his hardest to get me to understand the extent of the danger I could be placing myself in.

"I know that he's dangerous, which is why I still don't trust him. I'm not about to go out and show him my wings." I sigh loudly. "I'll just keep up the ruse of being a vampire. I'll get closer to him and find out as much as I can, and if for even a second I think I may be in danger, I will run away."

"You shouldn't have to do this, Piper. But if you've gotten this close without him figuring you out, then more than likely he never will, as long as you're careful." Dad states as he paces back and forth.

"Is this really the only way to get information, Michael? Can't we do something else?" Gabriel argues.

"I don't see any other way, Gabriel. This is our best bet to stay a step ahead of them." Dad replies.

"Yes, but how would you explain her relationship to Cam and you, Michael?" Gabriel inquires.

"I've already told him that we are in town on business. I told him that I had come along to hang out with Mason. I don't know how to explain you, Dad, but as long as I can stay at your place, Gabriel, they shouldn't suspect anything." Cam replies as he looks at Gabriel.

Gabriel nods his head.

"Of course, you can stay. You can as well, Michael. That way, we will all be close enough to keep our eyes on Piper and not look too suspicious." Gabriel recommends.

"What else have you told Alec, Piper?" He asks, turning his attention to me.

"He asked my age, and I told him I was eighteen, he looked at me oddly and mentioned it being strange that I had such a taste for angel blood, but I just explained to him that that had been the only blood that I've had. I think he bought into it, but he could still try to look into that bit of information." I answer.

"Is there anything else we should know of? Any details, whether big or small, might make a huge difference for us to pull this ruse off." Gabriel states.

"The only other thing that we may have to worry about is if I continue to have these blackouts. I can get closer to Alec, and I'm almost certain that I may even be able to keep him from actually doing his job." I confess.

"Don't do anything that you don't want to do, Piper. No one is forcing you to do any of this." Michael expresses while placing his hands on my shoulders.

I nod. "I know that. I want to help as much as I can. I know how far to allow him, and I won't let it get out of hand. He thinks I'm dating Mason anyway."

"That may become a problem since you broke up, Piper." Cam chimes in, reminding me of my mistake.

"That may work in your favor, Piper," Gabriel answers softly. "At least my son won't be looked upon as competition."

"That's true." Cam agrees. "You may have just saved him from trouble, Piper. If I know Alec, he would have played the game of getting you dirty. He already warned Mason when we were back at the school."

"He's definitely ruthless and cunning when it comes to getting what he wants." Michael agrees.

Chapter Sixteen

"Are you going out again tonight, Piper?" Hannah asks as she enters my room and sits on the edge of my bed.

"Yes, and no, you can't come tonight. It's too dangerous for you to be anywhere around Joel or me right now." I answer as I finish up the last curl of my hair.

"I know. Joel called me earlier to explain why we couldn't see each other." She sighs softly.

I stand, pressing my hands on my hips before I twirl around to show my sister my outfit. I went with simple black skinny jeans and a white lace tank top. To top it off, I had my favorite pair of knee-high black boots on.

"You look great, Piper," Hannah states while giving me a thumbs up.

"Thanks, Hannah. I wish you could go with me tonight. It's going to be weird showing up all alone." I sigh roughly.

Grabbing my black leather jacket, I slip it on.

"You'll be fine. Mason, Joel, and Cam will be watching over you." Hannah assures me as she stands, holding out my helmet.

"Thanks, Hannah," I whisper as I pull her into a hug.

I loved my sister even though we didn't always get along.

"You're welcome, Piper. Be careful tonight, okay." She replies as she leans back.

I nod. "I promise I'll be careful and keep my eye on Joel for you." I giggle as she blushes a bright red.

Patting her shoulder, I walk out of my room and quickly make my way downstairs, where I meet my mom sitting in the kitchen.

"You're leaving already?" She asks quietly.

I nod. "I'll be safe, Mom. Don't worry about me, okay." I insist.

I knew she would worry no matter what, especially since we had let her in on all of the details from earlier.

She was so scared to lose me.

It was my fear too. I didn't want to be torn away from my family.

Kissing her cheek, I quickly leave her behind. I could see the tears forming in her eyes, and I knew the longer I stayed, the harder it would be to leave.

"Love you, Mom," I yell back as I reach the front door.

"Love you too, baby girl." She answers back, her voice clogged with tears.

"I've got her, Piper. Go, do what you need to do." Hannah reassures me as she comes down the stairs.

I nod gratefully and then walk out the door.

Getting onto my bike, I leave with a heavy heart.

I didn't want to worry my mom, but this was my life now.

She had known before that my life would always be a bit on the crazy side, but we could never have guessed just how crazy and dangerous being me could be.

I was happy that this new life had brought my father back and that I had gained a brother, but the downfall was the part of having lifetimes to live while my sister and mother only had one.

It was something that I wasn't sure I could survive through.

Riding down the road, I look back to see Mason, Cam, and Joel pull out behind me in Mason's truck.

It made me feel a little bit better that they were close by, but for the most part, we had to act as if we weren't as close as we actually were.

****

I'm a nervous wreck when I finally pull into the parking lot of the club we favored.

Hopping off my bike, I glance around at the long line that had formed in front of the building. As usual, I bypassed the line, causing random people to yell out in anger and frustration.

Unfortunately, some of the people in line would never actually make it inside. Nevertheless, it was a plus to know people and to be what I was.

"Ah, there's my favorite girl. Are you here alone tonight?" Duke questions as I walk up to him with a bright smile.

"Yes, it's only me tonight. Is J.D. here today?" I question.

He nods as he holds out his arm. "I'm going on a break right now, so I'll see you in." He smiles down at me before glancing in the other bouncer's direction. "You're in charge until I get back, Leo."

The other guy, Leo, grunts as we walk past him and into the club.

"I still owe you a dance, don't I?" I smirk.

"Yes, you do, but I won't ask that of you today. I only want to have a drink with you, if that will be alright?" Duke replies.

"That sounds good to me, Duke." I agree as we make our way to the bar, where J.D. is already waiting for us.

"Do you want the same as usual, Piper?" He asks with a grin before setting an already-filled glass in front of me.

"You know me too well already, J.D." I laugh and take the glass in my hand as I wait for J.D. to pour Duke a drink.

Tapping our glasses together, Duke and I down our drinks in a single gulp.

"Thanks for the drink, Sweetheart." Duke grins as he then stands back to his feet.

He nods wordlessly to J.D. before leaving us.

"He must really like you. I don't think I've ever seen Duke take a drink with anyone." J.D. laughs.

I smile as I watch Duke's back disappear from view. "I still owe him a dance, though. I wonder if he will do that if he isn't normally one to be social."

"He might; you've got him coming out of his shell for the first time ever." J.D. answers.

"Is Cam coming in tonight?" He then leans in closer to ask.

"Yes, he is, but I can't be seen with him tonight, and if anyone asks, just tell them you don't know anything about us, okay," I whisper back.

"What kind of trouble are you in?" He asks with concern.

"There you are, Darling." Alec's voice rings out, and J.D.'s eyes go wide.

"That's the kind of trouble I'm in, J.D," I answer before turning to Alec as he approaches the bar.

"I didn't think I'd see you here again," Alec replies while glancing around before his eyes settle back on me. "Where's your boyfriend?"

"We broke up earlier," I confess.

"Why did you do that?" He questions softly as his hand strokes over my cheek.

"I told him the truth, I told him about kissing you, and it made him mad. He dumped me pretty quickly after that." I answer honestly.

"He's an idiot then, Darling. I'm sorry that I had a hand in your breakup. I shouldn't have pushed you into kissing me." Alec sighs.

"You didn't push me into anything I didn't want to do, Alec. I'm a big girl, and I know when to say no. So, don't blame yourself. Mason and I were growing apart anyway." I insist.

"I still feel bad about it," Alec whispers.

"Do you want another drink, Piper?" J.D. coughs out, breaking the moment apart between Alec and me.

"One more for me and one for him, J.D., thanks," I answer him.

He watches us for a moment before springing into action.

Handing a drink to Alec, J.D. stares deep into his eyes for a moment before speaking. "Remember what we talked about, Alec?"

Alec nods with a grin. "I remember, and you have nothing to worry about."

"I'm not even going to ask what that's all about." I motion between Alec and J.D.

"Honestly, I don't care. All I want now is to dance." I add and then gulp down my drink before standing to my feet.

"Dance with me, Alec?" I ask as I hold out my hand to him.

Grinning widely, he gulps his drink down before taking my hand in his to lead me out onto the dance floor.

With his hands on my hips and my arms around his neck, we sway to the slow song that's playing. His body is so close to mine that the heat radiating from him warms my own.

Leaning my head against his chest, I sigh as his heartbeat pounds in my ear.

"Is everything alright, Darling?" He questions softly, making his chest rumble.

"Everything is fine." I lie.

"Are you certain? You seem to be upset?" He presses.

"Nothing's wrong. I just want to forget about things for a little while tonight. Can you help me with that?" I reply.

"I can do that for you." He replies softly while lifting my chin before his lips brush across mine. "I will help you forget about all of your worries, Darling." He promises with another deeper kiss.

When a faster song begins to play, Alec spins me around so that my back is snuggly against his front. His hands start on my hips, but as the song progresses, his hand lands lower on my thigh while the other falls just under my shirt, barely skimming my skin.

"I can't get enough of you, Darling." He whispers into my ear as his lips trail down my neck.

I shiver as he reaches a particular spot.

His lips form a smile on my skin before he nips at the spot lightly with his teeth. "I want more of you." He growls out seductively.

"Tell me what you want, Alec?" I command.

"I want to feel your lips on mine, and I want to feel your legs wrapped around my waist once again." He answers as I turn in his arms to face him.

He opens his mouth to say something more, but his eyes travel to look over my shoulder.

"What is it?" I question quickly, growing alarmed.

"It's your ex. I think he may want to cause us some trouble." Alec answers softly.

"If he tries anything, I'll deal with it, Alec. This fight is between him and me, okay." I reply and search his eyes for his response.

"Fine, but if he even tries to lay a hand on you, I won't be able to control my actions," Alec warns.

"May I cut in?" Mason asks Alec as he approaches us.

"Why not just join us," Alec suggests over my shoulder.

Mason must agree because his hands quickly find my hips before he roughly tugs me back against his body.

Alec's eyes narrow as he grins in challenge.

This wasn't going to end well.

"I should have seen that coming. That's the last time you will get one on me, Mason." Alec laughs.

His hands snake around my waist just above Mason's hands.

I find myself squished between the two as they battle silently with looks and touches. They fight to see who can get the better reaction from me.

I moan as their lips leave trails on either side of my neck.

"You guys need to stop," I warn as my hunger takes hold.

When they don't listen, I growl out as my fangs descend.

Alec notices first and glances around to ensure I haven't been seen.

"You have to go now, Piper, before someone sees," Alec stresses as he pushes Mason's hands from me before he begins to pull me through the crowd.

Halfway through the crowd, someone snatches me from Alec's hand.

One second, I'm stuck in the middle of a never-ending crowd, and the next, I'm alone with a stranger in the supply closet back at the school.

"Who are you?" I ask quietly as I back away from the man.

"I'm Marcus." He answers softly. "...And I have to stop this. I can't sit back and watch you with those other two any longer. I don't care what the danger is. I'm giving your memories back of me so you know who should be holding you tightly."

"You're the one that keeps causing my blackouts, aren't you?" I question.

He nods while moving closer to me.

"Yes, and I'm sorry for that. I know I shouldn't have messed with your mind. That's why I'm giving everything back. I want you to remember me. I need you to know what we truly are." He replies.

My back hits the wall as he moves closer to me.

Once his body is pressed against mine, I look up at his face.

His eyes glow a bright red before pain washes over me. He grabs hold of my head, stopping me from looking away.

My mind is flooded with memories of him, of his wings, of my wings, and the way he had kissed me. Everything that had been taken away from me comes rushing back.

After a few moments, he steps back.

He grins while I search his eyes.

My hand rises a moment later to smack the grin off his face. I couldn't believe that he had messed with my mind so much.

His eyes widen in shock as he gently touches the side of his face.

"How could you do that to me? How could you do that against my will?" I bite out.

"I did it to keep you safe." He answers, pleading for me to understand.

"I am safe, Marcus. I'm safer without you around. That's exactly what this just proved to me." I reply harshly.

"You don't mean that. Please, Piper, don't make me leave you." He pleads.

"How can I be with someone who wouldn't think twice about taking away my memories? How do I even know that these are all you've taken?" I fire off while holding back the tears threatening to make an appearance.

"You can trust me. Those memories are all that I've ever taken. It killed me to do that to you, but you must understand it was for the best." He replies.

"Just take me back to the club, Marcus. After that, just leave me alone. I don't want anything to do with you. I can't even begin to ever trust you again." I cry, finally allowing my tears to fall.

I know I wasn't being reasonable, but I didn't like feeling betrayed.

I both loved and hated this man, or I should say, angel, in front of me, and I didn't know what to do other than to leave him.

I needed to be around someone that I could trust.

That's when it hits me. This must have been precisely how Mason had felt.

God, I felt like the worst person in the world.

I now understood why he hadn't forgiven me yet. It was hard to forgive someone you cared so much about.

Maybe, it would be better for Alec and his brother to find out what I truly was and have them take me away. At least then my family and friends wouldn't be in any danger.

"Just let me have one last moment with you, and then I will leave. I won't return unless you want me back." He answers sadly.

"Take me back now, Marcus," I argue, even as he leans forward before touching his lips to mine.

"I just want one last taste." He whispers before his lips caress mine.

His lips trail down to my neck, and I let out a low moan as his fangs sink into my skin. Acting on pure instinct, I lean in as his tongue laps at my blood and bite into his neck.

He stops for a moment as he lets out his own low moan.

Being connected like that, it was almost as if I could feel everything that he was feeling. It scared me a bit at first, but I just push his thoughts and feelings from my mind. I didn't want to listen to how much he wanted me to stay, how I was breaking his heart, and how he would miss every part of me.

It was a connection that I knew I was only going to have between us, but I still wanted to push him away.

For what reason, I didn't know exactly. Maybe I wasn't ready for that sort of commitment, or perhaps I couldn't trust him enough.

Either way, it causes me to pull away and stand back from him.

I slam my mind shut, much like Mason had slammed his door. I was putting an end to whatever it was that we had or could possibly have had.

I didn't want to give my heart away. I had to hide it like I had hidden it before. At least that way, I would never feel the heartbreak I had felt just moments before.

"Take me back to Alec, now," I command harshly.

I was done.

I shut myself off.

Chapter Seventeen

Back at the club, I search the crowd for Alec, Mason, or anyone I knew.

I needed to talk to someone, anyone.

Seeing Marcus's face just before he left me alone had almost torn down all the walls I had built.

I could literally feel his heart breaking.

Giving up on finding anyone in the crowd, I decide to try my luck at the bar.

"There you are. Everyone is looking for you, Piper." J.D. states as I sit down in an empty seat.

"Where are they now? I was just looking for them." I question.

"They're all over the club, but I'm sure they'll come back here soon enough." He answers while sliding a drink in front of me.

"I need something stronger than that to forget all of the stuff I know now, J.D," I answer as I stare down at the liquid in the glass.

"What do you mean by that?" He questions while looking at me oddly.

"It means that I know what you are, and I know now how you've been watching over me." I grin, and his jaw drops for a moment. "I should thank you for that, by the way."

"I take it Marcus is the reason that you went missing?" He inquires with a raised brow.

"Yes, and it won't be happening again. He's gone for good now." I growl out before taking the drink and gulping it down.

J.D. watches me for a few moments before nodding to himself while pouring me another drink.

"What happened to you, Darling?" Alec whispers as his arms suddenly wrap around me possessively.

"I don't know, one minute, I had a hold of your hand, and the next, I got lost in the crowd." I lie easily.

"It won't happen again." He promises with a kiss on my cheek.

"No, it won't." I agree before I gulp down my second drink.

J.D. pours me more, and I swallow two more glasses before I stand and then lead Alec back to the dance floor.

As I dance with him, I get flashes of anger from Marcus that I must continually push out of my mind. I didn't want to think at all. I just wanted to feel free.

I wasn't about to let him ruin my rather good mood. I was enjoying my dance with Alec far too much to allow his emotions to bother me.

His hands felt wonderful on my body.

"I really wish you could feel how jealous these people around us are. It's completely intoxicating." Alec whispers into my ear as our eyes float over the people around us, watching our every move.

I could feel what he was feeling, but I couldn't tell him that.

Turning in Alec's arms to face him, I glance over his shoulder to see Cam, Joel, and Mason watching me from the bar.

"I want to get out of here." I insist while still watching the others.

"Why do you want to…?" Alec trails off as he spins us and spots who I had been looking at over his shoulder.

"Where do you want to go?" He then replies as he grins back down at me.

"I want to go somewhere where we can be alone," I answer seductively.

"Let's go to my place, then." He suggests.

I nod. His place was going to be perfect.

As we turn to leave, I'm forced to grab my head with my hands as a loud voice rings out.

The voice begs me not to leave. I glance around the room, noticing that no one else seemed to have heard anything that I just had.

Alec was looking at me oddly.

Shaking my head, I sigh before standing up straight and grabbing his hand again.

"Let's go," I state before he can ask me what is wrong.

There couldn't be something wrong with me, right?

"Did you drive here by yourself, Darling?" Alec questions as we exit the club.

I nod. "Yes, I did, but it's probably not the kind of vehicle you would expect me to drive," I answer.

He raises one of his brows, intrigued. "What kind of vehicle would surprise me?" He questions curiously as we walk through the parking lot.

When we stop by my bike, his eyes glance from me to it over and over until a smirk crosses his face, and his eyes finally settle on me. "I am surprised. I took you for more of a tame girl, but it seems you have a bit of a wild side after all."

"Do you know how to drive one? I've had too much to drink to be driving." I ask.

"I can." He answers while holding out his hand for the keys, which I hand over without a fight.

"Just be careful; she's my baby." I laugh as he throws his leg over it and then waits for me to do the same.

"I'll be careful." He promises as he starts the engine and then revs it to a loud roar.

I smirk and wrap my arms around his waist.

Within seconds, we are flying down the roads as I hug tighter to him, feeling his chest rumble with laughter.

It was like he was a little kid again.

I knew he had to be decades old from how Michael, Cam, and Gabriel talked of him.

It was good to hear his loud laughter. It showed me a piece of him that I'm sure he wouldn't have normally shown anyone else.

As we ride through the town, I quickly notice that he wasn't taking me to some house or apartment. Instead, he was taking us to the park, the one that I had flown in.

Parking in the lot, I climb off the bike and wait while Alec climbs off after a moment.

"Why did you bring me here, Alec? I thought we were going to your place." I question curiously.

"I wanted to bring you here to talk. This is the only safe place to do so without anyone else hearing." He answers while pulling me towards the trees.

"What do you want to talk about?" I question nervously as we come to a stop.

Placing both of his hands on my shoulders, he looks deep into my eyes.

"I know what you are, Piper." He admits.

I laugh nervously while shaking my head. "What do you mean? I already know that you know what I am, Alec."

"No, you don't know that I know that you're an angel. That you're a one-of-a-kind creature that could destroy or heal our world." He answers as I stare at him in shock. "You're what I was sent to hunt, Piper."

"How...how...did you figure it out?" I stutter in fear.

"I put a few puzzle pieces together. It's what I do." He smiles gently.

"So, what happens now? Do you take me to whoever wants me? Do you kill me?" I question as I glance down at my feet.

"I keep you hidden." He answers softly, causing my head to whip up to look into his eyes. "I don't want to lose you, not now. You're too good to be taken to the place that wants you."

"You would defy those people for me?" I question while searching for the truth in his eyes.

"I would do anything for you, even if it meant defying my very own brother." Alec declares.

His eyes never leave mine as he speaks.

I felt as if I could truly trust him, but at the same time, a part of me still feared being tricked.

"Would you be willing to die for me?" I push.

He nods without hesitating. "Yes, I would die for you, Piper."

"What are you going to do with your brother?" I question next, needing to know how far he was willing to go in order to keep my secret hidden.

"I will tell him that I haven't found you yet. I will make up some excuse. I'll send him on a wild goose chase if I have to. I swear that I will keep you safe." He vows.

"I believe you, Alec," I whisper while laying my head against his chest.

We stand there in silence for a few moments before I pull back to look into his eyes with a grin.

"Can I see your wings?" I ask.

"Of course you can, Darling." He answers with his own grin.

He guides me through the trees before letting me go to shuck off his shirt.

I watch wordlessly as he reveals cut abs and a broad chest. Of course, he would look good. I don't know what I had been expecting. Every angel I had seen so far was gorgeous.

When his wings unfold, I gasp at their size.

They had to be three times the size of my own.

"I know what you're thinking. You're wondering why my wings are so large, aren't you." He states, and I nod.

"They're this large because of the lives that I have taken. The more damage a dark angel does, the larger his wings will grow. So, when we go into battle with each other, it shows the other angel just how dangerous the other is." He explains.

"So, you've killed people?" I ask quietly.

He nods. "Yes, I've killed both guilty and innocent humans."

"Do you ever regret killing them?" I wonder aloud as I walk closer to touch his wings.

Even though his feathers appeared disheveled, they were surprisingly soft beneath my fingertips.

"Yes, I do. I feel their deaths on my hands every day. It's only moments when I'm with you that I forget, even if it's only temporary." He admits as he closes his eyes and tilts his head to the night sky.

I don't know why I ask my next question. It just comes out of me as if it's from another being altogether.

"Do you want forgiveness for your actions?" I ask as I continue to touch his wings.

"If it were possible to ask for that, then I would say yes. It would feel good not to carry around all of the guilt." He breathes out while glancing back at me.

Closing my eyes, I run my hands along his wings to where they connect with his back. They flap a little as I tighten my grip while a strange energy courses through them and into my hands.

I find the sensation invigorating as his energy fills me.

Taking my hands away after a few moments, Alec falls to his knees, panting as if he had just run for miles without stopping.

"What did you just do to me?" He pants out while looking back at me.

"I took away your burdens," I answer easily as I walk around to face him.

As he flaps his wings, they rise higher on his back. They still looked just as large as before but not weighted down as they had been.

"How can you do that?" He questions as he stands to his feet.

I shrug and step closer to him. "I don't even know how I knew to do any of that. It all just kind of happened."

"You're amazing, Piper, truly amazing," Alec whispers as his lips find mine.

Pulling back moments later, I grin widely and then take a step back.

Shrugging off my jacket, I turn away from Alec and pull off my tank top, leaving me in only my bra.

My wings unfold, and this time it is his gasp of awe that I hear.

I smile shyly as I look back at him.

"Can I touch them?" He asks.

I nod and watch as he slowly makes his way closer.

Just as his fingers are about to touch them, the same voice from before screams in my head, causing me to fall to my knees.

"Get the hell out of my head," I growl in anger as I clutch my head in my hands.

"What is it?" Alec asks as he touches my shoulder, causing the voice to yell again.

When his hand leaves my shoulder, the voice in my head stops yelling.

I pant in relief as I stay still, wondering if it will come again. If only I knew how the voice was screaming in my head, then maybe I could block it.

Standing back to my feet, I turn to face Alec, not caring that he could see me in my bra. Reaching out, I touch him, half expecting the voice to yell out, but it thankfully doesn't.

"What are you doing?" Alec questions with a soft laugh.

"Just trying something. Can you touch me?" I question, causing him to tilt his head in confusion.

"Just do it, please. I have to figure out why my head feels like it's going to explode." I explain.

He nods before reaching out to take hold of my hips.

With his fingers only inches away, the voice screams out in my head again.

I step back and close my eyes while gritting my teeth as everything becomes clear. The connection I had felt with Marcus, the new bond I had felt.

It was him screaming in my head.

He didn't want anyone else touching me.

"You have got to be kidding me," I mutter in disbelief and anger.

"What's going on, Piper?" Alec asks, breaking into my internal thoughts.

"It's nothing." I insist.

Once again, I move closer to him. I was determined to figure out a way to block Marcus from my mind. I wasn't about to let him control my life.

Leaning up, I press my lips to Alec's lightly at first. I grin when I don't hear Marcus's voice.

As I deepen the kiss, Alec's arms circle my waist as he pulls our bodies closer together.

Marcus's voice yells in my head once again, and I work hard to block it as I continue to kiss Alec.

It almost becomes unbearable until, all at once, it disappears. I grin, proud that I had finally found a way to block him.

"You are simply amazing, Darling." Alec grins against my lips as he gazes into my eyes.

"So are you, Alec," I reply with another deep kiss.

"I'm far from amazing, Piper. I'm still not a good person to be around, and as much as I don't want to admit it, I should let you go." He whispers sadly as he pulls away a moment later.

"Please, don't let me go, Alec. You're the only one keeping me from drowning in despair right now. I need you." I plead.

"I wasn't going to let you go. I just said that I should." He chuckles lightly before continuing. "I'm a selfish jerk who could care less about what I should do. Being with you feels right," Alec answers with a cocky smile.

"Good, you had me scared for a moment." I laugh out with him.

Leaning my head against his bare chest, I grin as his hands circle me and lightly brush against my wings.

Being with him did feel right. At least, that's what I kept telling myself.

In truth, being with Alec felt wrong in every single way. His touches, his kisses, they all felt wrong. I was being the selfish one, keeping him around even when I knew I would eventually break his heart.

I didn't care because he made me feel loved, and that's all that mattered to me at this moment. I could trust him, and I could be with him easily without having my heart shattered.

"We should get you home, Darling." Alec states, his chest rumbling with every word.

I nod and look up at him. "Take me home with you?"

"Are you sure you want to go to my place?" He questions, and I nod with a smile. "Alright, but let me warn you now, it's a bit of a bachelor pad, especially since it's only me and my brother living there."

"That's fine. I don't mind a little mess. I just don't want to go home yet. I want to spend just a little more time with you." I reply.

Alec smiles down at me as his hand caresses my cheek.

"How did I get so lucky to find you?" He questions absently before his lips once again brush against my own.

Breaking apart, he bends down to pick up our discarded shirts.

He holds out mine to me, and I take it as I will my wings away.

I watch silently as he folds his wings away and pulls his shirt over his head. His muscles bulge and ripple as he moves, mesmerizing me.

"Enjoying the view, Darling?" He laughs out, and I nod unashamed while biting my lip. "I know I'm enjoying my view." He replies as he gestures toward my bra.

I snort in amusement before slipping my own shirt over my head.

"Let's go before we end up staying here all night." I flirt as I take hold of his hand, pulling him towards my bike.

"I wouldn't complain about spending the night here with you, Darling." He laughs as he follows me.

"I didn't figure you would, but if anyone comes looking for me, this will be one of the first places they will check. I'd rather not have them see us in a compromising position." I answer, causing Alec to stop.

"Does that mean what I hope it means?" He asks as a wide grin spreads across his lips.

"You'll find out if we ever make it to your place," I reply with a wink.

He quickly jumps into action, practically dragging me the rest of the way to my bike.

I laugh the entire way. "For being bad, you sure do make me laugh a lot."

"I won't be making you laugh when we get back to my place." He answers seriously as he climbs onto the bike.

His promise makes me shiver as I climb on the back and wrap my arms around him. I didn't know if what I was doing was smart. I mean, I was ready to be with someone, but I was still scared.

I didn't know if once we got to his place, I would be able to go through with it. I didn't want to make him angry with me, and I certainly didn't want to feel pushed into something I would later regret.

I would have to play this out moment by moment.

I would go with my instincts.

And if I had to, I would walk away from whatever we had.

Chapter Eighteen

Arriving at Alec's place, I'm surprised to discover that he lives above a small store in town.

I don't know why I figured him to live in a huge mansion. I just thought that someone like him would live in an elaborate house, not some dinky apartment.

Hopping off the bike, Alec takes my hand and leads me up a rickety old set of stairs.

Looking back, he must notice my confusion because he stops halfway up the stairs. "This isn't what you were expecting, is it?"

"No, to be honest, I was expecting a lot more," I answer honestly.

He only shakes his head with a wide grin.

"I do have a better place than this where I live when I'm not working. I promise you; it would blow away any ideas of what you're thinking right now." He gestures to the run-down building. "This place just helps us blend in a little better. We don't want people asking how two young guys can afford a huge house alone without holding regular jobs."

"That makes more sense." I giggle as we continue on our way to his door.

He jiggles his keys as he turns the lock and then pushes the old door open.

The inside is dark, so I wait by the door as Alec makes his way inside to find a light to turn on.

When the light finally flickers on, I step inside, only to stop when I hear another girl giggle.

I glance toward Alec in question, but he only shrugs in response.

A door opens inside, and Sid walks out in only a pair of low-riding jeans.

"You're finally home. It's about time. I thought you'd stay out with that vampire all night." He laughs. "Does that pretty little mouth taste as good as I thought?" Sid rambles on as I stand still in the doorway staring in horror at Alec.

"Sid…" Alec tries to talk, but Sid cuts him off.

"I brought home a real girl if you want to try her out. It's been days since you've had any good action, and I know that girl hasn't given you any since I can still smell the stench of her virginity on you." He continues. "How is she even a vampire? I mean, what idiot would turn her and not get anything out of it? I would have at least taken what I wanted from her."

"Sid, would you just stop." Alec spits out.

"You need to get laid, Alec. You're moody." Sid laughs, still not getting Alec's hints to just shut up.

"Hey, Jayden, get your cute butt out here." Sid suddenly yells back to the room that he had just exited.

I am forced to watch as she comes out wrapped in just a thin sheet.

I shake my head as I step out of the apartment, as Alec pleads for me to stay with his eyes. I couldn't; I wouldn't stay.

Just as I'm about to turn to leave, Jayden turns in my direction with wide eyes. A second later, her eyes narrow as a smug grin crosses her lips.

"Hey, Piper, what are you doing here?" She asks, faking innocent.

Sid turns around to spot me and then curses before he turns back to Alec. "Crap, I didn't know you brought her home, Alec."

"I was trying to tell you that, but as usual, you wouldn't shut your damn mouth." Alec snarls as he walks past his brother and Jayden.

"Please understand, Piper. I didn't know he would be here with her." He tries to explain, but I shake my head.

I should have known this was too good to be true.

I couldn't trust anyone.

As my anger builds, I feel all of those burdens that I had taken from him earlier build back up in my hands. I push them out in front of me as he moves closer.

"You didn't deserve to have me take all of your burdens away, and you don't deserve me," I growl out as I shove him hard, allowing the power to flow from my hands back into his body.

He slumps to the floor, panting, the heavy weight of his sins weighing him down again.

"Piper, please don't leave me." He pleads while gazing up at me.

"Go enjoy her because we will never happen. I hate you." I bite out before flipping his brother and Jayden off.

Sid snarls back at me as I turn and then jump from the top of the stairs.

I was stupid to believe that things would finally work out for me. I couldn't believe that I had been so close to giving myself away to the wrong person.

Rushing to my bike, I quickly hop on and start it. I glance back to see Alec running toward me, trying to stop me from leaving, but I don't give him a chance.

In a rush, I take off down the road.

Looking back once more, I see him standing in the road. His eyes widen with horror just before a wall slams into me.

In moments everything goes dark as my bones break and shatter.

My eyes open and close as I try my hardest to stay awake. My body before me was twisted in such ways that any normal human would never be able to survive.

Glancing over, I spot the wall, or should I say the truck, that I had slammed into.

The driver gets out panicked as he rushes over to my body.

"I didn't even see her until it was too late." He cries as Alec and Sid rush over.

"It's going to be okay, man. It's not your fault." Sid talks calmly to the driver while steering him away from the wreckage.

"Piper, can you hear me?" Alec asks as he moves closer to me.

"I'm still here," I answer as blood pours from my mouth.

Suddenly, a shrill scream pierces the air.

"Oh my god, is she still alive?" Jayden questions as she moves closer.

"Sid, get her out of here," Alec orders his brother as he kneels next to me.

"I'm sorry...." I start to talk, but he stops me by placing his fingers on my lips.

"No, don't even say it." He growls out as a tear escapes his eye. "Just tell me how I can help. How can I fix this, make you better?"

"You can't," I answer while searching the skies, hoping to spot Marcus.

I was hoping and praying that this time he would finally save me.

"I don't believe that. There has to be something that I can do." He pleads.

Sid appears by Alec's side before moving him away from me for a moment.

"We have to get her out of here, Alec. If the humans find her alive, they'll become aware of us and her kind." His hands slide under me as he picks my broken body up.

I choke out as more blood pours from my mouth.

As Sid stands, he looks over to Jayden and then back to Alec.

"You know what you have to do, Brother. Do it quickly." He commands roughly.

Alec nods once before Sid turns and rushes me away from the crash and back into their apartment.

"Tell me how I can save you, Piper." He demands while placing my broken body down on a soft bed.

"I don't know how, Sid," I answer softly.

"Yes, you do. I can't let you die. If I do, Alec won't be the same." He pleads.

"Just let me die," I whisper as the pain and darkness finally take over.

Moments later, I become alert once again.

My eyes stay closed even as I fight to open them.

"Did you do what needed to be done?" Sid questions.

"I did, and I made it as painless as possible. So, no one will ever know that she wasn't actually the one involved in the accident." Alec answers sadly.

"I know you hate killing the innocent, but you had no choice. No one can find out about our world. If they knew angels, vampires, and werewolves were real and not just myths, they would hunt each one of us down." Sid stresses.

"I understand that Sid, and that's why I did what had to be done, but it doesn't mean that I liked it. I'm nothing like you, Brother." Alec growls out.

"Can we heal her?" He asks, changing the subject.

"I don't know how. The only thing we can do is give her our blood and help straighten her bones out as they begin to heal." Sid replies.

"Then that's what we'll do. I can't let her die, Sid. I just can't." Alec sighs roughly.

"I know that, Alec. We will do whatever we can." Sid promises.

As my eyes finally flutter open, Alec caresses his fingers lightly over my cheek.

"There's my girl." He whispers.

"I'm still here," I reply while looking over at Sid.

"I'm sorry about all of this, Piper. I really am." He apologizes as he bows his head in shame.

"Yes, you are, which is why you're going to feed her first while I clean her up." Alec snarls as he stands to his feet before walking away.

I watch as Sid's shoulders slump.

"You two killed Jayden, didn't you? You put her in my place?" I question softly.

He nods as his eyes meet mine. "Yes, we did. It was the only way to keep our kind safe."

"You're not as strong as you'd like to have people think, you know." I laugh out with a cough.

"No, I guess I'm not always." He chuckles as he moves closer to me.

Holding out his wrist, he places it against my mouth.

"Drink, Piper. Take whatever you need." He commands.

I bite into his wrist roughly.

He yelps and I grin against his skin as I drink his blood.

"I guess I deserved that." He chuckles.

When he begins to grow pale, I fight to stop myself. I didn't want to take too much of his blood and kill him.

As much as I hated to admit it, I needed him.

Once I finally manage to pull away, Alec returns to the room with washcloths and a bucket in his hands.

Handing a wet cloth to Sid, they both get to work cleaning me up. I let out tiny yelps as they hit tender spots all over my body.

They both work to get bones in place and to re-break the bones that weren't healing correctly.

Just like when I had fallen from the sky, I knew this would be a long, complex recovery process. I couldn't help but wonder if I would make it this time, though.

I wondered where Marcus was and why wasn't he coming this time. He had to know what had happened. He had to have felt it.

To be honest, this was probably what I deserved for pushing him away, and he wasn't going to save me when I needed him the most.

"What are you going to say to my family?" I choke out as Alec washes the dried blood from my face.

"We can't tell them anything. They're just going to have to think that you ran away." He answers.

"That's not who I meant, Alec," I reply gruffly.

He shakes his head roughly as he glances over at his brother.

"You should just tell him the truth, Alec." I sigh.

"I can't, Piper. I promised that I wouldn't tell anyone." He argues.

"Tell him so you can bring Cam, Mason, and Joel here. They can help heal me better than just the two of you. I'm going to need a lot of blood." I plead uselessly with him.

I could see the fear in his eyes. He knew something terrible would happen if he exposed my true identity to his brother.

And I could understand his fear, but it didn't matter to me anymore. I was tired of hiding, and I would tell Sid myself if it got me the help I needed.

All I had to do was get a moment alone with him.

"I won't let you tell him, Piper." Alec bites out as if reading my mind.

"You can't be by my side forever, Alec," I argue.

"I can try. I won't allow you to put yourself in danger like that." He declares.

"I put myself in danger the first day I met you in the men's restroom." I laugh.

"So, you finally remember that, huh?" He questions with a raised eyebrow.

"I remember a lot of things," I answer softly while closing my eyes. "I wish I could forget most of those things, though."

"Why would you want to forget again?" He asks softly.

"Because I need to forget how being in love felt," I answer before reopening my eyes.

He nods in understanding. "I get it. You wish you could erase your past and start over."

"Exactly, I want to be able to start new." I sigh softly.

"I think we all wish for that at some point in our long lives, Piper." Sid chimes in, breaking into our conversation.

We all become quiet, lost in our own sad thoughts.

Chapter Nineteen

After three days of constant healing, my body had almost healed completely, but I was still sick and too weak to even move from the bed.

"What's wrong with her?" Sid questions no one in particular as he paces back and forth in the tiny room.

"She's completely healed, so why can't she move?" Alec asks while looking at me with concern.

Both of them hadn't left my side.

They had taken it upon themselves to fix me the best that they could.

The problem now was far from their control. I needed Marcus to finish healing. I needed his blood and our bond to bring me back from the edge of death that I was still clinging to.

"She needs something that you're not telling me, Alec," Sid presses.

"He doesn't know what else I need, Sid. If he did, do you really think he would just be sitting here watching me die like this?" I snap back at him.

"Then you need to tell us what you need, Piper." He demands.

"I can't tell you that," I answer softly before closing my eyes.

"Yes, you can, but you would rather die. Admit it, Piper. You want to die, don't you?" He growls out furiously.

I don't answer or make a sound.

"Then die, Piper. Just die already so my brother can move on." Sid then spits out before leaving the room, slamming the door behind him.

I open my eyes to Alec and watch as he opens his mouth to say something, but then stops when we hear a loud bang come from the room where Sid had just gone into.

Alec peeks out the door and curses.

"What is it?" I ask.

"It's Mason, and he looks ticked." He states.

"Where is she, Sid? I know Piper is here." Mason growls fiercely.

"She's not here," Sid growls back.

"She is here. I can smell her scent. Now, tell me the truth." Mason demands.

"You're wrong. She and my brother ran off together." Sid lies.

"You're lying. She would never just run away from her family." Mason argues as something else smashes against the wall with a loud crash.

"Just tell us where she is and why Jayden was riding her bike." Cam's voice bites out this time.

Just as Alec steps back from the door, it bursts open to reveal Joel. His white wings out behind him, making him appear more dangerous than I had ever seen him.

"There you are, Sweetheart." He grins as he walks into the room, giving Alec a disapproving glare.

"I'm fine, Joel. Just stop Mason and Cam from hurting Sid, please." I plead softly.

"Seriously, you want me to stop them? Sid did this to you, didn't he?" Joel questions.

"No, he didn't. I did this to myself, Joel. Sid and Alec have been taking care of me." I explain.

"Really? They've been taking care of you?" He asks as he glances at me oddly.

I nod.

"Fine, I'll stop them." He huffs out a breath before leaving the room.

"They helped her? Are you being serious, Joel?" Mason growls out loudly.

It's quiet for a moment before I hear their footsteps coming toward the room.

Cam and Mason walk through the doorway and glare at Alec before kneeling beside the bed.

"What happened, Piper?" Cam asks while taking my hand in his.

"She took off on her bike. She was angry at my brother and me. I tried to stop her, but she pulled out right in front of a truck." Alec answers for me.

"So, it wasn't Jayden that had been riding your bike?" Mason questions while gritting his teeth together.

"No, it wasn't her. I was the one who crashed." I answer softly.

"So, you thought it would be a great idea to kill a human to put in her place?" Cam growls as he stands to his feet to face Alec.

"It's the only thing I could do. I couldn't let the humans find her; you know that." Alec answers with his head bowed in shame.

I knew it had bothered him.

He hadn't wanted to kill Jayden. I didn't even think Sid did, either. They did it in order to save me, though.

It would have been nothing but trouble if someone had found me alive.

"You should have gotten us. We would have helped you." Mason growls lightly while still looking at Alec as he takes my hand.

"Why are you still sick?" He asks in a softer tone as he turns his full attention toward me.

"You know why," I state while glancing over his shoulder at Sid.

"You need his blood to heal?" He questions just loud enough for me to hear.

I nod and then sigh roughly. "I need more than just that, Mason."

"Can I talk to them alone?" I ask while turning my attention to Sid and Alec.

They nod before leaving me alone in the room with Joel, Cam, and Mason.

"We haven't seen or heard from Marcus, Piper. I don't know if we can even find him in time." Cam whimpers.

"You have to try. If you don't, I will die this time." I answer my brother as I lift my hand to touch his cheek.

"Why, what changed?" He questions while placing his hand over mine.

"I formed a bond with him before he left. I could feel what he felt and hear what he was thinking. I was foolish and selfish when I blocked him from my mind. I can't seem to get that bond back, and I've tried everything I can think of." I confess as my vision blurs.

"How long do we have?" Joel questions this time.

"I don't know. Every minute that goes by, I grow weaker." I answer him.

"We will find him, Sis," Cam promises as he wipes my tears away.

"Alec knows what I am, by the way. He figured it out, but he hasn't said a thing to Sid, so keep quiet around him, okay." I add.

"We'll be careful. Can we trust Alec, though?" Mason stresses.

I nod confidently. "Yes, I believe that we can. He has done everything in his power to keep me safe. He's been lying to his brother, so I believe we can trust him."

"Does Alec know about Marcus?" Joel adds.

"No, he doesn't. I haven't said a word about him." I answer.

"Good. Now the question is, can we move you, or would you just rather stay here with Alec?" Cam presses.

"I think she should stay here where they can protect her." Mason insists, surprising us.

"Are you sure?" I question while searching his eyes.

"Yes, they've done a good job of watching over you so far." He trails off as he closes his eyes for a moment. "It would be better for you to be with someone you care about just in case we don't return quickly enough."

"You will return in time, Mason. I know you will." I reply as another tear escapes from my eye.

I didn't actually know how much longer I could hold on, but I would try my hardest to stay with them until they came back, with or without Marcus.

Standing to their feet, Mason and Cam look down at me sadly, each of them holding tightly to my hands, not wanting to let go.

With only a nod, they both let go and then exit the room, leaving Joel and me alone.

"I will keep them strong for you, Piper, and I'll make certain we are back in time. I want them to have a chance to say goodbye if they have to." He promises me.

"Let's hope it doesn't come down to a goodbye, Joel," I reply softly.

"Let's hope, pray, and cross our fingers and toes that it doesn't." He chuckles, trying to make light of the situation.

"Be safe, Joel, and bring him back to me," I whisper, becoming serious.

"I will. I'll bring him back kicking and screaming if I have to." He promises before taking my hand in his.

He leans down to place a soft kiss on my cheek before moving away, holding onto my hand until the last moment before he lets go and disappears back through the door.

As it shuts, I allow my tears to fall.

It had felt as if I would never see any of them again. Their last looks might have actually been our goodbyes.

This life had been nothing but cruel.

"Piper, Babe, why are you crying?" Alec asks as he rushes back into the room.

"I'm crying because I just said goodbye to them. I know I won't see them ever again." I sob as he pulls me into his arms.

"You're going to make it through this, Piper." He vows confidently.

"No, I won't, Alec. I'm sorry, but I will not be able to hang on." I whimper.

"Yes, you will, Piper. You will, not because of my brother, but because you don't want to leave everyone around you." Sid states as he walks back into the room.

"You won't make them deal with your death, Piper. I won't allow it." He vows.

"I don't think I have a choice in this, Sid." I cry as Alec rocks me in his arms.

Sid moves closer to touch my cheek.

He smiles, and I close my eyes for a moment.

"Yes, you do, Piper. You always have a choice." He whispers. "You can sit back and die, or you can fight for life until you take your last breath. Either way, it's your choice; you just have to make the right one, the one that's right for you."

"I know I should think of it like that, but all I can think of is how much better life would be for everyone around without me in it," I reply honestly.

"None of us would be better off without you here, Piper." Alec answers in a whisper, his voice clogged with tears. "Don't make me have even more regrets to carry, Piper." He pleads as his tears finally fall.

"Can you set me up, Alec?" I ask suddenly.

He nods and then does as I ask. He sits me on the bed but has to hold me steady.

I turn my attention to Sid. "Can you hold me up so Alec is free to move?"

He nods before coming over to my side quickly.

"What are you doing, Piper?"

Alec questions as he looks down at me.

I smile softly and twirl my finger for him to turn his back to me.

"Show me your wings, Alec," I command.

"No, Piper. I won't do this." He growls as he turns to face me.

"What is she trying to do, Alec?" Sid questions while looking between both of us curiously.

"I'm trying to take back something that I should've never done. I'm fixing one of my wrongs." I answer as I twirl my finger again for Alec to turn around.

"Now, show me your wings, dark angel," I growl out the command this time.

Before he can even take off his shirt, his wings rip through, obeying my command.

"Holy…" Sid whistles out.

"Piper, don't do this." Alec pleads as my hands float across his wings to where they meet his back.

Just as before, my hands lock on in a tight grip before his power flows into me. All of his sorrow and all of his burdens flow out from him.

This time I make sure to take it all away.

His wings become lighter and shrink slightly in size as I continue to hold onto him.

"Piper, please stop," Alec begs.

"What are you?" Sid questions as I finally release my hold on Alec's wings.

He looks between Alec and me for a few moments before I see all of the puzzle pieces clicking into place inside his mind.

"She's what we've been looking for this whole time, isn't she?" He asks Alec.

"Yes, I am," I answer for him.

"Why didn't you tell me that you already had her in your grasp?" Sid growls out in frustration.

"I fell in love with her, Brother," Alec answers simply.

"Where is the other one? Where is your mate?" Sid barks out at me as he slams my body back onto the bed.

His black wings unfold as Alec tries to fight his way to me.

"He isn't coming. I don't even know where he is." I answer truthfully while looking straight into his eyes.

"Why wouldn't he come for you?" He questions.

"I pushed him away and told him to never come back," I answer calmly.

"Why would you do that to your mate?" He asks, surprised.

"I did it for your brother," I answer in a whisper, causing him to look at me oddly.

Taking my left arm in his hands, he grunts as he breaks the bone.

I groan as the pain slices through my body.

"Sid, stop now. You're going to kill her." Alec cries out as he continues to fight to get to me.

"You don't get it, Alec. She's not going to die. Her mate would never let that happen. So, all we have to do now is draw him out." He replies. "Then our job here will be done, and we can return home."

I cry out as he breaks another bone in my arm.

"Please, stop," Alec begs.

"Learn to deal with this, Alec. She isn't yours anyway; she never was. She's been leading you on this entire time. She was lying to you." Sid growls out.

"I wasn't lying to him, Sid. I really do care about him. That's why I forgave him." I argue.

Gritting my teeth, I hold back my cry as Sid breaks yet another one of my bones.

"Now, tell me where we can go so your mate will find you," Sid growls in my face.

"The park. If he wants me, he will come to the park." I spit out at him.

The park was one of the few places I knew that Marcus would come for me. I also knew it would be the best place to get away from Sid.

And even if I didn't get away, it would be a good place to die.

The park held a lot of my happiest memories.

"Then that's where we'll be going," Sid replies before he lifts me in his arms and then storms past Alec.

The look on Alec's face would forever be scorched into my mind. It was a look of fear and desperation.

He was going to do something stupid; I just knew it.

Chapter Twenty

Charging out the door, Sid quickly takes flight with me still in his arms.

Alec is quick to follow.

Sid was on a mission, and there was no changing his mind, which is probably why he and Alec were the best team of hunters out there in our world.

I was probably the only one who had ever come between the two.

"I will watch you die if he doesn't come for you. I have never failed a job, and I'm not about to just because you decided to toy with my brother's mind." Sid warns as we fly closer to the park.

"It's not me that will be dying today, Sid," I reply while smiling sweetly at him.

"That's not what you said five minutes ago, Sweetheart." He laughs out at me.

"Yes, but I never said you wouldn't die with me," I reply seriously.

"You can't kill me; you have too much heart." Sid taunts.

"I can't, but that doesn't mean that Marcus won't. He wouldn't hesitate for a moment." I threaten.

"Ah, so is that your mate's name, Marcus?" He questions, and I nod.

It takes him a few moments to think the name over as I watch his eyes for the simple sign I was hoping for.

As it crosses his eyes, I grin triumphantly to myself.

I knew he had heard of Marcus before. They knew what he was and just how dangerous he was too.

He knew my words were true, and it put a healthy dose of fear into him.

Touching down in the park, Sid tosses me to the ground. I hit with a hard thud, and my breath is knocked from my chest.

As I curl into a ball on my side, Alec rushes to my aid.

"Did you really have to do that?" He growls up at Sid.

"Grow a new backbone, Brother." He demands harshly before lifting his foot and slamming it into my side.

I cry out as my ribs crack.

Alec holds onto me tightly as I take blow after blow from his brother.

"Come out...come out...wherever you are, Marcus. Come save your mate before I have the pleasure of killing her." Sid sings out loudly into the night sky.

"He's not going to come without others, Sid," Alec warns.

"He can come with as many as he wants, but he won't do anything to us as long as I have her in my grasp," Sid replies.

I grasp onto Alec's torn shirt to pull him down closer.

"Alec, I need you to warn Mason. Can you do that for me?" I plead, and he nods while looking panicked. "If you want to save me, you have to get them. Marcus will come alone if he comes at all." I explain, and he nods again.

"I'm afraid to leave you, Darling." He whispers as his hand caresses my cheek.

"Don't be afraid, Alec," I whisper before pulling him in for a kiss.

Pulling away reluctantly, he squeezes my hand tightly before standing to his feet and then quickly flying off.

"Where the hell does he think he's going?" Sid growls out as he walks back over to my side.

"I sent him away. He doesn't need to watch you kill me." I spit out.

"He's become such a coward since he met you. I, for one, will be glad when you're gone so I can get my brother back." He bites out before kicking my side again.

A bone slices into my lung with the blow causing blood to begin pouring out from my mouth as I struggle to breathe.

"Where's your stupid mate?" He then growls out as he searches the sky.

"Sid, he isn't going to come for me. You might as well kill me now." I push.

"He will come for you. You underestimate your bond, Piper." He insists confidently. "The question isn't whether he will come. It's what will make him come for you."

"What doesn't your mate like others to do to you?" He then questions.

"He won't care what you do, Sid. He isn't going to come for me," I scream at him, believing my every word.

I didn't believe for a moment that Marcus would come for me. He would have by now if I meant anything to him.

Kneeling beside me, Sid grabs my neck before slamming my head into the ground. My head spins as everything goes in and out of focus.

"What is it going to take?" Sid growls out in frustration.

"He's not coming, you idiot. He could care less about me. Can't you see that? I wouldn't have been allowed to be with your brother if he had cared." I laugh out harshly.

He frowns at me for a few moments, taking in my words until I see a spark in his eyes. His frown turns into a grin as his hand loosens its grip on my neck.

"I understand now, and it's not violence that will bring him. Oh no, that's not what he fears at all." Sid barks out with a laugh.

"Is it, Marcus? You don't care that I beat her half to death." He yells into the sky.

He grins widely while looking down at me with hungry eyes before he continues. "But he does care who touches you and how they touch you."

"Don't do it, Sid," I warn uselessly.

"Why not, Piper? Are you afraid to feel a real man?" He taunts.

"You're no man, Sid. You're nothing but a cruel, vicious animal." I reply with a growl.

"I'll take that as a compliment, Piper." He laughs as his hands move to rip my shirt off. "It's too bad my brother can't be here to do the honors. I bet taking your virginity will be fun, and I bet taking you from your mate and making you mine will be even better."

"Please, don't do this, Sid. You can have me, just not like this, please." I plead as he then tears at my torn and tattered jeans.

As his hands finally touch the bare skin of my inner thighs, I cry out. I continue to cry as his hands roam over every inch of my exposed flesh.

I didn't want this, especially not with him.

"Please, stop," I beg as he lifts off me just enough to start unbuckling his pants.

"I won't stop. Not until you're either mine or until your mate shows up." He growls.

"Marcus, please." I cry out as a last resort.

I was far too weak to fight against Sid.

Thankfully, just as Sid is about to make true to his threat, a large shadow moves to hover over us.

Sid moves to look up and laughs.

Mason, Cam, Joel, and Alec descend on us as quickly as they can, but at the last moment, Sid covers us with his wings.

They were no match for him, though, and he easily holds them all at bay.

"Is that all you've got?" Sid laughs out in amusement. "Have you switched sides now, Brother?"

"I did the second you thought you could take her away from me, Sid," Alec growls.

"That's really sweet, but she's going to be mine for good in just a few moments, and then you'll still lose her, Brother." Sid laughs in reply.

"I'm not going to let you do that without a fight, Sid," Alec warns.

"Go ahead and fight then, little brother." Sid challenges.

He moves against me again, and I begin to fear that this is how my end will come. At least, I hoped it would end if he got his wish.

I would rather die than become his.

Mustering every ounce of strength that I have left, I fight against Sid. I fight until he's positioned over me just right.

I grin triumphantly at him just as he realizes his mistake.

I jerk my knee up right into his manhood, causing him to fall to his side while gasping for air.

"Did you really think I wouldn't fight, Sid?" I laugh in his face as I roll to my side to look him in the face.

"You forget that even though you won that battle, I won't give up that easily." He insists before jumping back to his feet, a bit unsteady.

He leaps at me as I try to roll out from under his wings. His body slams into mine, stopping me.

I groan as my ribs break further and puncture my lung again. I cough up more blood as I pant for my next breath.

"It seems I've broken you even more, Sweetheart." Sid laughs manically as he resumes his earlier position on me.

"Just do it already. Just kill me." I growl out before I spit blood into his face.

"Not before I get a good feel of you first, Piper." He groans as he moves against me again.

I close my eyes, waiting for the worst.

Suddenly, his weight is lifted off of me. I gasp in shock as I open my eyes to see Marcus holding him up above his head.

"She. Is. Mine." He yells out before he throws Sid into the trees nearby.

He takes my hand in his while kneeling beside me.

"I'm sorry I'm late, my love." He whispers to me as his hand touches my cheek.

"Don't ever leave me again, Marcus," I growl softly.

"I won't." He promises as he leans down, exposing his neck to me.

Brushing my lips across his neck, I elicit a low moan from him before I bite down.

After only a few moments, his fangs pierce my skin. His body moves over mine protectively while his wings create a canopy to cover us.

I sigh in relief as my bones begin mending and healing quickly.

Pulling away, I take a deep breath of much-needed air.

"Feeling better?" He asks while searching my eyes.

I nod. I was feeling tons better.

"I'm sorry about pushing you away, Marcus." I apologize softly.

"Don't worry about that now." He answers. "Let's just get out of here."

Standing to his feet, he holds out his hand to me, and I take it.

Once I'm on my feet, I try and fail to cover myself while I glance around at my brother, Mason, Joel, and Alec.

Mason shucks off his shirt quickly and hands it to me. I slip it on, thanking him wordlessly with my eyes.

"I'm taking her home. I'll meet you all there." Marcus states seconds before we are engulfed in bright light.

A moment later, we appear in my room.

I sigh in exhaustion before walking over to lie down on my bed. "Come lay with me for just a little while, Marcus." I plead softly as I pat the bed next to me. "Before everyone else gets here."

He nods and then lays down next to me before wrapping his arms around me, holding my body snuggly to his.

I finally felt complete.

"I missed you," I whisper.

"I missed you too, Piper." He replies quietly.

"Why didn't you come to rescue me faster?" I ask.

"I was caught up in another battle. Your friend back there was smarter than he let on, and he double-crossed his brother long before we ever knew." He explains.

"So, he knew what I was this entire time?" I whisper.

"No, he didn't, not until he staged that accident to happen." He replies.

"He staged all of that?" I ask in shock as I turn in his arms to face him.

He nods. "Yes, he did, and I'm sorry that you ended up caught in it all, but he kept staying one step ahead of me."

"Can we trust Alec?" I inquire.

"I want to say that we can, but only time will tell with that. The bond of brothers runs deep within our blood." He answers honestly.

"I really hope we can trust him." I sigh roughly before turning back around in his arms. "He would be a huge asset to have around."

"Yes, he would, and he would protect you with his life. That means a lot to me." Marcus agrees.

A moment of silence surrounds us before I speak again. "Please, don't ever leave me again."

"I won't, not even if hell tried to rip me away." He answers with a tender kiss on my cheek.

I turn my face towards him before he growls seductively, seeing the hunger in my eyes. I wanted him. I needed him after what had happened today.

I needed to feel him, all of him.

"Are you sure about that, Piper?" He questions softly while moving to hover over me.

"I need you, Marcus," I whisper fiercely before kissing him deeply.

The door to my bedroom opens, and I groan as my father, mother, and Gabriel walk in.

They all gasp in shock at the compromising position we were in and cover their eyes.

"I get that we're interrupting, but we need to talk about what has happened and what our newest threats are Marcus," Gabriel states calmly.

"Just ten minutes. Can't they leave us alone for ten minutes?" I whisper just loud enough for Marcus to hear.

"I would need more than just ten minutes, Angel." He replies with his own whisper. "We can begin again after we talk to them, okay?"

"Fine, I guess I can wait until then," I grumble before untangling myself from his arms.

"I will make it worth the wait." He promises before standing to his feet in front of my parents and Gabriel.

"Let's talk while Piper gets dressed." He insists before motioning towards the door.

I watch as they all file back out of my room.

With a quick glance back at me, Marcus winks before leaving, shutting the door behind him.

Not wasting a moment, I rush into my bathroom and quickly hop into the shower. I needed to get myself clean since I hadn't had a shower in days.

I could still feel the dried blood on my skin from the wreck.

Scrubbing my skin raw, I continue to stand in the shower even while the water begins to run cold.

When I can't take the frigid water any longer, I get out and wrap a towel around myself before I quickly make my way into my room to gather some fresh clothes to put on.

I opt for a comfy pair of bootcut jeans and a faded grey tee shirt.

After slipping on my socks, I brush my wet hair out before deciding that I'm ready to face my family.

I couldn't wait to get this over with, so I could finally have my alone time with Marcus.

Once I'm ready, I nod at my reflection in my mirror and force a smile before heading off to find everyone downstairs.

Making my way through the house, I find everyone standing around Marcus, Michael, and Gabriel, who were sitting down at the kitchen table.

"What kind of attack should we be looking for next?" My father asks Marcus as I walk into the room.

"I'm not sure. I've been one step behind Sid this entire time. I honestly don't know what lengths he will go to in order to capture us." He answers while I move over to him and then sit on his lap as everyone watches us.

"You smell better," Marcus whispers in my ear.

"You still need a shower, stinky." I laugh as I hold my nose.

"Alec, do you have any clue what your brother will do?" Gabriel questions as he turns his attention to Alec, standing against the wall watching Marcus and me.

"I had no clue that my brother had even crossed me. I never thought he was capable of that, so, no, I don't know what he has up his sleeve, but it probably won't be pleasant." Alec answers without his eyes ever leaving me.

It gives me an uneasy feeling, but I shrug it off.

"Go with your gut on that one, Piper," Marcus whispers into my ear, breaking into my inner thoughts.

I nod and turn my head to lay it on his shoulder.

"Do we know how much information Sid has?" Michael asks next.

"We have to assume that he knows everything at this point. He knows what I am and what Piper is. He also knows that we need each other." Marcus answers.

"He also knows that he can take me away from you right now since we haven't had the chance to…you know," I add bashfully.

"How did he come across that information, though?" Gabriel questions absently.

"What's our next move?" Cam pipes into the conversation.

"We wait for him to move since we're at a complete loss here," Michael replies. "We must protect Marcus and Piper at all times, though."

"Aren't we supposed to be able to kill angels? Shouldn't they be afraid of us and not trying to capture us?" I question.

"You would think that, and yes, we can kill them, and they should fear us, but they don't. They only have one thing on their minds, and that's how they can use our powers if they catch us." Marcus answers as he strokes his hand over my hair.

"That, and you have too much of a heart to kill, Piper. It's your one weakness, and Sid knows that." Alec adds.

"So, then, someone needs to teach me how to fight." I proclaim.

"It takes years to learn, Piper. It's not something that you can learn overnight." Cam snorts in amusement before sighing loudly. "But if someone needs to teach you, I'm the best since I'm the only one here who has been in a battle between angels."

"Good, now, onto the next thing we need to discuss." Gabriel looks at me sadly. "We must explain why that young girl was found dead with your bike, Piper. The police have been searching high and low for you, and we have been lucky so far to keep them off your case, but we're going to need to come up with a good, believable story to explain why she would have had access to your bike."

"I can't believe she's dead," I whisper as I glance up at Alec, who still hadn't taken his eyes off me.

He had killed her, and it made me wonder what else he could be capable of doing. He had plenty of secrets that I didn't know about.

"It's unfortunate, but I agree with what Sid and Alec did. They had no choice but to cover the accident up." Michael states.

Glancing over at Mason, I notice that he, too, had taken notice of how Alec was watching me.

Standing up from Marcus's lap, I walk over to Mason.

"Can I talk to you alone for a minute?" I ask, and he nods.

We walk out into the living room, and I stop to look back before leading him upstairs to my room.

Closing the door, I lean back against it and sigh.

"We need to keep an eye on Alec. Something isn't right with the way he has been watching me." I stress.

Mason nods his head in agreement.

"I was wondering if you felt off about that. He hasn't been right since we left the park." He replies.

"Do you think he's going to try something?" I ask, becoming worried.

"I definitely think he will, but he's going to be smart about it." He answers.

"Keep your eyes on him for me, okay, and let Cam and Joel know that something isn't right too. I've had an off feeling about him since I sat with Marcus." I sigh again. "But maybe this is all in our heads, I mean, I pretty much dumped him for my ex, and I haven't said a word to him since. If I were him, I'd be pretty upset and angry with me too."

Mason nods thoughtfully. "That could be true, but he could also be one of those types that plot revenge to get back what he wants, and if what he wants is you, then Marcus is the one that will be in the most danger."

"That's what I'm afraid of." I sigh.

"I'll keep him in my sights, Piper. If he tries anything, I won't hesitate to stop him. So, try not to worry too much, okay." He insists.

I nod. "Let's get back downstairs. I think Marcus needs to talk to me some more." I state as his voice fills my head.

"How do you know that?" Mason asks curiously.

I laugh while pointing to my head. "I hear voices in my head."

"You're not supposed to listen to those voices, Piper. When will you ever learn?" He teases.

"It's hard not to listen to them when they whisper promises into your head," I smirk.

"Don't tell me stuff like that, Piper. I don't even want to know." Mason laughs as we exit my room and then begin to make our way back downstairs to the others.

I stop at the top of the stairs when I notice Alec standing at the bottom.

"Go ahead and talk to him. I'll be watching from the doorway, and, if you can, let Marcus in on the conversation so he can be aware of what's happening." Mason whispers into my ear before leaving Alec and me alone.

"Are you okay, Darling?" Alec asks as I move down the steps to join him at the bottom.

"Yes, I am now. How about you? I know this has been a lot to take in…" I trail off, not exactly knowing what to say.

"I don't know how to feel exactly." He answers honestly.

Just then, Marcus joins in on our conversation through our connection. I don't know how I knew he was there, but I did.

"Just tell me, be honest with me, please." I press gently.

"Piper, I just went from you being mine, then almost being forced to watch my brother rape you, and now you're suddenly with that guy in there. I don't know how I should feel. I don't know if I should be mad or upset or grab you and run." He explains with so much pain lacing his voice.

"Is he your mate like my brother said?" He asks sadly.

"Yes, he is," I answer softly. "I'm sorry about all of this, Alec. I really am."

"You're breaking my heart, Darling. Do you know that?" He whispers.

I sigh softly. "I do, I honestly do, Alec. I never meant for any of this to happen. Hell, I sent him away so that I could be with you."

"But… Come on, Piper, there's always more to it." Alec pushes.

"Couldn't you feel that things weren't exactly right between us? Didn't it feel like things weren't how they should have felt?" I press.

He shakes his head. "No, I thought everything was perfect. I guess I was a fool to believe you might have loved me."

"I did; I do care about you, Alec. I always will. Just promise me that you won't do anything stupid. I still want us to be close." I reply, pleading with him not to turn his back on me.

"I won't do anything stupid, Piper. I still want to be close to you too." He replies and grins widely before he kisses my cheek.

Without saying another word, he walks away abruptly.

I stand alone for a few moments in confusion.

Could it have really been that easy? I shake my head. No, it couldn't, not if the other person really did care. I had learned that from when I had broken Mason's and Marcus's hearts.

"Crap," I mutter before walking back into the kitchen.

As I sit back down on Marcus's lap, he wraps his arms around me protectively.

"Everything will be alright, Angel." He whispers into my ear, trying to comfort me.

I nod as he kisses the top of my head.

"I think that's enough talk for today. Marcus and Piper need time alone to rest." Gabriel states for everyone to hear. "I can't even imagine what you've been through these last few days, Piper, but be assured we will keep you two protected."

"I know you will, Gabriel," I reply softly.

"Let's get some sleep, Angel," Marcus states as he smiles at me.

I nod in agreement.

Standing up, he carries me in his arms out of the kitchen and then up to my room.

"Do you think we will ever be able to sleep in peace?" I ask as he lies me down on my bed.

He shakes his head. "We will never be completely at peace, Angel, but as long as we have each other, things won't seem as bleak."

"I can't wait until we get past this threat." I sigh as he lies down next to me.

"I can't wait to finally get you alone." He laughs as he mocks a look of shock. "Oh wait, we are alone, in bed, and now we can finally finish what we started earlier."

I laugh as he moves over my body before he begins to nuzzle my neck.

"I love you, Marcus," I whisper.

"I love you too, Piper." He replies wholeheartedly.

Kissing me senseless, we both tear at each other's clothes wanting to be as close as possible, our hands touching every inch of each other's skin.

It felt good to finally have him here with me, and it helped me relax slightly to know that we were safe.

"I need you, Marcus." I moan out as his lips trail down my neck.

"Are you sure?" He asks as he moves to look into my eyes.

"Absolutely; I need this, Marcus. I need to feel you completely." I almost plead.

"I need that too. I've needed this for a long time now." He admits.

"I know, and I'm sorry for pushing you away. It was a stupid thing to do. I see that now." I apologize.

"You weren't ready for this before. That's why you pushed me away. I understood your feelings then, and that's why I didn't put up much of a fight." He replies with a grin as he brushes a strand of my hair behind my ear.

"I knew there had to be a reason you didn't." I laugh softly.

His grin widens. "I knew you would come back to me. You already knew it in your heart that you were mine."

"I am yours, Marcus," I reply before kissing him.

"And I'm yours, Piper." He replies before he kisses me back passionately.

A shadow in the room catches my eye, and I turn my head, quickly becoming alarmed.

"What is it, Angel?" Marcus asks while lifting himself over me.

"I don't know," I whisper as I squint into the darkness.

Looking back to Marcus, my eyes go wide to see Alec standing over us. I don't even get a chance to react before he shoves a pipe straight into Marcus's chest from behind.

Marcus's eyes go wide as he looks down at me in horror.

"Crap." He mutters as he pushes himself off me so he wouldn't fall on top of me and impale us both with the pipe.

He then falls lifelessly down to the floor with a hard thud.

Sid appears next to Alec, and I gasp as I try to cover myself with my sheet.

"It's about time, Brother. I was beginning to wonder if you did switch sides on me." Sid laughs as he picks up Marcus's now lifeless body.

"What are you going to do to us?" I whimper in fear.

"Marcus is the only one they wanted, Darling. So, you can do whatever you want now." Alec snorts in amusement before he watches Sid jump from the window.

"You lied this whole time?" I whisper.

"Yes, I did. How else would I get the great Marcus into a weakened position? You were just a fun toy in the process of doing my job." He laughs as he stalks toward me.

"I will kill you both for this, Alec," I vow.

"Please do, Princess. I would love to see Sid destroy you." He laughs out again while getting into my face.

With one well-placed head butt, I knock him down just as Mason and Joel burst through my door. They grab Alec and haul him to his feet as Gabriel and Michael rush in next.

"Where's Marcus?" Gabriel questions.

"Sid took him. Alec is a traitor." I reply quickly.

"Let's take him away so we can get some answers, Mason," Gabriel growls as he grabs Joel and Mason's arms.

They flash away leaving me behind with my father.

"Get dressed, Piper. We have to hide you." Michael orders before leaving me alone in my room.

Not knowing what else to do, I quickly get dressed before making my way downstairs, where Cam is waiting for me with open arms.

I go to him and begin sobbing into his chest.

"How do we get him back?" I cry.

"I don't know yet, Sis, but we'll get him back no matter what it takes." He promises.

"We have to. We have to get him back." I whisper as my emotions clog my throat.

"And we will, Piper. We will get him back, but first, we must prepare you for a fight." Michael states as he walks into the room.

I turn to face him as I wipe my tears away.

I was more than willing to do anything to get Marcus back, anything at all.

"Where do we start?" I question eagerly.

"We start by teaching you how to kill," Michael answers with a rough sigh.

The Angels Evermore

To Be Continued…

Other Books by: Raven K. Asher

Completed Series

The Story of Alexis Rose Series

The Angels Evermore Series

Among the Dead Trilogy

Eden One Series

The Vampires of Linbridge Series

The Onyx Wolves Series

The Winter Fae

Series In progress

The Chosen Series

Life's a Fairytale Collection

Love and Blood Series

The Dragons of Willow Creek

The Angels Evermore

Singles

Losing Levi

Stolen (When Worlds Collide and Stars Align)

When Tomorrow Never Comes

Damage Me

Colton Clark (A 'Damage Me' Novella)

Crash

Love Unexpected

Rock Me

Reverse Harem Singles

Forbidden

Finding our Pack

Rockin' It

Burnt Skies

Savage

About the Author

Raven K. Asher is the author of the Reverse Harem series The Vampires of Linbridge. She is also the author of, Sci-Fi series Eden One and the Paranormal Romance series, The Onyx Wolves. In addition, she has written Young Adult singles such as Losing Levi, When Tomorrow Never Comes, and Love Unexpected. Raven was born and raised near a small town in Northern Ohio. Soon after graduating high school, she moved to Chicago, Illinois, where she lived for five years before moving back to her hometown in Ohio. Shortly after moving back, she met and married her wonderful husband. They have been married for fourteen years and have two amazing daughters. She has always had a love for writing and has made her lifelong dream of becoming a writer a reality. When she isn't reading or taking care of her pets and kids, she is diligently writing the many stories trapped inside her head. Raven's passions are romance and horror, but she additionally enjoys sci-fi and fantasy stories. Her favorite stories to write are her post-Apocalyptic tales.

Thank you for Reading.

Raven invites you to please leave a review, giving your thoughts and reactions to this story.

The greatest support you can give to any independent author is to leave them a review, so if you could take a moment of your time to leave a review on the site where you purchased this book, it would be greatly appreciated.

I appreciate your support.

Raven K. Asher

You can find updates on upcoming stories, teasers, release dates, special insights, social media links, and the occasional giveaway at Raven's official Website:

www.ravenkasher.com

The Angels Evermore

Sneak Peek

For:

BookTwo

Captured

The Angels Evermore Series

By: Raven K. Asher

The Angels Evermore

Chapter One

"**Y**ou need to kick higher with your left foot, Piper," Cam demands as we practice different fighting styles.

We had been at this every morning and afternoon for two months. I couldn't believe it had been that long since Marcus had been taken from me.

"I *am* kicking higher, Cam." I huff out before trying the kick once again.

Other than practicing my fighting skills with Cam, I hadn't done much else.

Every part of me wanted nothing more than to find and rescue Marcus, but as far as I knew, no one had found or heard anything about him yet.

He had pretty much vanished into thin air.

Since there wasn't anything that I could do, I was focusing all of my energy on fighting. It was the only thing keeping me from falling into a pit of despair.

As Cam blocks my kick again, I spin and catch Mason's other brother, Derek, off guard. I slam my other foot into his chest, and he falls back on his butt with an approving grin.

"Very nice, Piper, but you left your back wide open to attack." He laughs as Cam grabs hold of me from behind.

With my arms pinned behind my back, I was rendered utterly useless.

"I can't take any more of this today." I pant as I slump forward from exhaustion.

Cam and I had been practicing for well over three hours so far today.

"You're not done yet, Sis. We need to push your limits. When you're fighting in a battle, it won't matter how tired you feel; it will be a matter of life or death." Cam argues.

"What's it even going to matter? No one even knows where Marcus is." I huff out, allowing my body to fall limply to the ground.

This was a regular routine for me. I had thought about giving up nearly every day for the past two months.

I couldn't get past the hopelessness that had burrowed deep into my heart.

"Don't give up yet, Piper. Dad will be coming back soon with Mason and Joel. Hopefully, they will have some useful information for us." Derek insists while casting a shadow over me.

"Are they bringing Alec back with them?" I ask curiously.

"I believe so." He answers with a nod.

"Did they get him to talk at all?" I question while squinting up at him.

"I don't think they did, Piper." He answers with a sigh.

"We should let Piper kill him, or at least act like she is. I bet he would talk then." Cam growls out.

We were all frustrated with Alec.

Ever since we had captured him, he hadn't said a word. Instead, he had literally taken a vow of silence.

We had tried everything to get any kind of information out of him, but we were consistently met with little success.

I had been hoping that the mind-reading angel that Gabriel and the others had taken him to would have gotten something, but again, we probably weren't going to be that lucky.

"At this point, I'm all for just killing him." I clip out seriously.

"You're going to have to wait and see what my father found out before you get all bloodthirsty, okay." Derek laughs.

Cam shakes his head and laughs loudly as my eyes change from their normal baby blue to a deep dark red as my hunger rears its ugly head.

"You did it now, Derek. You just had to say the B-word, didn't you?" Cam chuckles before Derek slams his palm against his forehead.

"I didn't even think." He whispers while watching me approach him.

"Well, at least now we can get a little extra practice in," Cam states right before he slams into me from the back, knocking me off of my course.

"What are we going to play this time, keep away or hide and seek?" Derek laughs playfully and dodges my outstretched arms as I charge after him again.

Frustrated with their games, I stand straight and spread my wings.

The sunlight felt wonderful on my feathers.

I grin up at the sky for a moment before bending down to push off the ground.

With my wings spread, I take flight, soaring far above the ground and over Cam and Derek.

"It looks like it's going to be a game of keep away, Cam," Derek calls out as he then pushes off the ground next, his large black wings unfolding mid-jump.

He laughs as I dive for him, only to miss him by mere inches.

After a few minutes of chasing my brother and Derek around, I begin growing even more frustrated.

The hunger quickly takes complete control, causing me to turn feral. I sniff the air trying to pinpoint a scent strong with blood.

Searching around for the source, I spot Mason standing on the ground with his wrist held up in the air. He must have cut himself so that I would smell his blood.

Grinning mischievously up at me, he spreads his wings before taking flight.

I don't hesitate to swoop down after him.

It's a mistake.

I should have known that they would all turn this into another training exercise.

As I continue on my path, driven by hunger toward Mason, Joel comes out from nowhere and slams into me.

We both fall to the ground with hard thuds.

I fight as he pins my arms down against the grass easily, snapping my teeth at him as he laughs playfully.

"Who set you off this time, Piper?" He questions while glancing around as the others land nearby.

"Who ticked my girl off?" Joel then asks curiously.

Derek steps forward a moment later with a bashful look on his face while raising his hand. "It was me."

"Has she even fed from you yet, Brother?" Joel inquires with a raised brow.

Derek shakes his head. "No, she hasn't. She's refused to feed at all since you guys have been gone."

Joel turns his attention back to me. "You need to feed, Piper. It's probably why you're so easy to take down."

"I don't need to feed from anyone, Joel." I lie even though I continue to try and bite him.

"You're not a very good liar, Piper." Joel snickers before turning his attention to his brother. "You need to experience what it's like to feed her, and learn how to control her, so she doesn't kill you."

Joel then sighs as he looks back down at me. "Now is as good as any time to learn since she's famished."

"It's too dangerous for him to try that right now, Joel." Mason disagrees while stepping forward. "I'll feed her. He can learn later."

I watch him closely as he kneels next to me before holding out his arm.

Joel glances from me to Mason with a mischievous grin before he releases me abruptly.

Mason's eyes go wide as I jump up to my feet. I quickly flip him over onto his back before sinking my fangs into his neck.

Wanting to gain control, he quickly flips us over, so I'm on my back, and he's on top.

Almost instantly, I retract my fangs and push against him roughly as flashes of Sid pinning me down at the park flood my mind.

"Get off of me, please get off of me, Sid." I cry out, suddenly stuck in another place and another time.

The heavy weight lifts off of me, but I still cry out. I wanted nothing more than to be back at home in Marcus's arms, where I felt safe.

Just being back home with my mother and sister would have been nice, but I was stuck half a world away in Ireland at one of Gabriel's homes.

It was the one place where we could be ourselves since there wasn't anyone, human or other, around for miles.

"Piper, Sweetheart, please come back to us. You're safe; Sid isn't here." Joel reassures me, trying to break into my thoughts.

"Just let me go, please." I whimper as I curl myself into a ball on my side.

"Derek, get her inside. Mason, Joel, and Cam, I need you over here to help." Gabriel commands.

"Piper, I'm not going to hurt you, but I have to get you inside, okay," Derek explains as he places my arms around his neck before lifting me to carry me, much like you would a child.

Laying my head against his chest, I whimper as he carries me inside the house and then into the living room, where Flynn stands up from his seat.

He was a new addition to our little group but an important part to me.

He was a spunky Nephilim who, much like me, was just learning who he was since his father had abandoned him for unknown reasons.

"What happened to her?" Flynn questions with his Scottish accent.

"I don't know; I think she had another flashback," Derek answers as he hands me over to Flynn.

Once in his arms, I look up into Flynn's soft green eyes and then sigh softly as he calms my frantic heart.

As a light angel, Flynn had a unique ability to calm people around him as long as he was in contact with you somehow. He had helped me several times when I would wake up in the middle of the night screaming, or like now when the past took over my present.

"Thanks, Flynn," I whisper as he sits down in his chair, still cradling me.

"You know I'd do anything to make you feel better, sweet Lass." He replies and grins softly down at me while running his free hand through his scruffy red hair.

"I wish you could take away my memories like Marcus could. At least then we wouldn't have to deal with me freaking out like this anymore," I whisper while closing my eyes.

"I wish I could too, Lass, but I can't." He sighs as he begins to rock me in his seat.

The tips of my wings drag over the hardwood floors making a faint swooshing sound.

A few moments of silence with just the swooshing of my wings go by until we hear footsteps tapping on the hardwood floors coming towards us.

"How is she doing, Flynn? I heard she had another spell on the field just a little while ago." My father, Michael, asks as he stands over us.

Opening my eyes, I look up at him and smile. "I'm fine, Dad. It wasn't so bad this time." I answer as I will my wings away before climbing off Flynn's lap.

"Just tell him the truth, Lass." Flynn urges as he watches me.

"Okay, fine, it was bad," I admit as I bow my head, feeling like a failure.

If I couldn't begin to get past my nightmares, how would I ever face whatever dangers would come when it was finally time to rescue Marcus?

"It will get better with time, Piper. Just keep working on blocking the fear out. No one can hurt you here." Michael sighs softly as he picks my chin up to look at him. "You're stronger than you think, Daughter. I know you can't see that now, but you are."

"Did you get any useful information?" I question, changing the subject as I pull my face away from my father's grasp.

I begin to pace across the floor as I wait for his response.

He shakes his head. "Nothing that will help us to find Marcus, but we did get something that may help us get him to finally talk."

"And what did you find out?" I ask while turning to give him my full attention from across the room.

He brushes his hand over his face roughly before looking up at me. It was apparent that he didn't want to answer my question.

"He will only talk to you, Piper. That's all we got from him." He sighs before continuing. "You don't have to talk to him if you…." He trails off as I raise my hand to stop him.

"If he wants to talk to me, then fine, he can talk to me while I kill him slowly," I growl out as I storm past my father and Flynn.

I was on a mission.

And I was furious.

Just as I reach the door leading downstairs into the dungeon that Gabriel had constructed to contain Alec, Mason, and Joel rush up the steps to stop me at the top.

"Get out of my way," I demand with a snarl.

Joel shakes his head roughly. "No, you're not going down there like this."

"I have to go down there, Joel," I argue. "If this is the only way he's going to give us information about where Marcus could be, then I have to do this whether I like it or not."

"We heard what you said, though, Piper, and we can't risk you killing him out of anger. He's the best chance we have to get any valuable information." Mason tries to reason with me.

"I won't kill him, Mason. Instead, I'll make him wish he was dead," I reply while smiling sweetly.

"Just let her go downstairs and talk to him, boys. There isn't anything that can happen if we're all down there with her." Michael chimes in from behind me.

I glance back and smirk as Cam and Derek join him.

Looking back to Mason and Joel, I watch as they nod before moving out of my way.

Pushing past them, I leap down the staircase, skipping all of the steps, before making a mad dash into the room where Alec was being kept.

Mason and Joel curse loudly as they race after me.

Once I reach the room, Alec stands to his feet and then moves towards the bars.

I smile sweetly as I move over towards him before grabbing hold of his neck through the bars of the cell in which he was being held.

He chokes as I lift him just enough to where his feet were no longer touching the ground. His eyes then go wide as he sees the red in mine.

I wasn't holding my hunger or anger back.

I wanted nothing more than to rip his throat out and lap up his blood as he died, but Mason had been right. I couldn't do those things because if I did, it possibly meant losing our only lead to finding Marcus for good.

Growling fiercely, I toss him easily into the bars behind him. He crumbles to the floor just as the others join me in the room.

With my thirst raging and clawing at my throat, I turn and grab the closest angel near me. Within a split second, I'm drinking down their delicious blood.

I didn't care who it was; I was just too hungry.

Moaning softly, I bite harder, eliciting a small groan from the angel I was holding onto tightly.

"Piper, you need to stop," Mason demands suddenly from behind me.

I ignore him.

"Damn it, Piper, you need to stop. Derek hasn't done this before and doesn't know how to stop you properly." Mason growls as his hands wrap around my waist to pull me away.

I growl again while unfolding my wings in order to push him away from me.

Letting out a frustrated growl, he rushes me, trying to get past my wings, but I effortlessly block him at every angle until he stops.

"Derek, you need to stop her. Remember how I showed you?" Mason stresses as he gives up his attack on me.

A moment passes before Derek moves.

Derek's hand slips between us before he grabs my neck tightly, cutting my air off so I can't continue drinking or breathing until he lets go.

Everything comes back to me, and I pull away before Derek drops down to the floor to his knees.

Alec laughs out from behind me as if everything that had just happened was just some big joke.

"That was utterly priceless, Princess." He snorts. "You so badly wanted to kill me, but you nearly killed one of your own instead."

"Enough, Alec. I don't want to hear anything else come from your mouth unless it's information about Marcus." I snap while turning to face him.

"What are you going to do if I refuse to tell you?" He questions while grinning smugly.

I move closer to the bars and close my eyes as I control my pheromones to overwhelm him. I would get him to talk in any way that I could.

Opening my eyes, I smile as he moves closer while his eyes widen in fear.

He couldn't help himself even though he didn't want to come closer to me. He knew just how dangerous I was, but he was helplessly under my control.

Slipping my arm through the bars, I grab his arm and guide it through with mine, pulling his body against the bars.

Shaking his head, he manages to release himself from my spell, but it's already too late. I had a firm hold on him.

He pulls against my grasp, cursing, trying to get away from me uselessly.

He was trapped.

"Now, are you going to tell me what I want to know, or will I have to play dirty?" I question him with a sadistic grin.

He visibly gulps before shaking his head. He wasn't going to talk.

"Piper, what are you going to do?" Michael questions behind me nervously.

I don't speak as I stare deep into Alec's eyes while trailing the fingers of my free hand across his forearm before abruptly digging them into his skin, drawing blood as he cries out in pain.

Stopping for a moment, I question him again. "Are you going to talk now?"

He shakes his head again as he bites his lower lip.

Again, I sink my fingers deeper into the muscles and tendons of his arm. He cries out in pain while fighting against my grasp to free his arm.

"Tell me what I want to know, and I'll stop," I state simply.

He nods vigorously. "I'll tell you anything you want to know, but not with any of them here, and I want you to come inside this cage with me."

That was close enough to what I wanted to hear. At least we were getting somewhere.

Releasing his arm, I turn to face the others in the room, who were sharing the same look of concern.

I sigh roughly. It was going to be hard to convince them to leave us alone, but since it was going to be the only way to get Alec to talk, I had to convince them that I would be fine.

Anyway, I was a big girl. I could easily take care of myself.

Of course, they weren't going to think that way.

Chapter Two

"No, absolutely not. I'm not about to let you walk into that cell with him alone. You have no idea what he actually wants to do." Mason argues with me while pacing the floor in the kitchen. "I highly doubt that all he wants to do is talk to you, Piper."

"I can handle anything he can possibly do," I argue.

Stopping in place, Mason shuts his eyes before rushing towards me, knocking me down to the floor at Joel's feet.

With his body on top of mine, I scream as flashes of Sid race through my mind.

Tears instantly pour from my eyes as I fight to stay in control.

It was useless.

"What if he was to do something like this to you, Piper?" Mason asks softly before pushing himself back off of me.

Whimpering, I roll to my side and curl into a ball. He had easily proved his point. If Alec did anything like that, I would be in big trouble.

"Did you really have to do that to her, Mason?" Joel clips out.

"She's weak, Joel, and I had to prove that to her. If he would try something like that, she needs to be able to fight back, not crumble and weep." Mason stresses.

Again, he was right; I needed to be stronger.

"She's been through so much, Mason, don't you see that? You can't blame her for falling apart on us." Joel clips out.

"I just wish that I was enough to keep her strong," Mason admits softly.

"But you're not, and I don't think that's going to change, Mason. So, you'll have to commit to being her friend and nothing more." Joel replies gently. "That's what she needs right now, a friend, not someone who wants to show her every weakness she has."

"I don't think I can do that," Mason replies shortly before leaving the room.

Cursing lightly, Joel kneels beside me and takes me in his arms before standing back to his feet.

Cam walks in as I snuggle into Joel's arms for comfort.

"What happened?" He asks.

"Mason happened. He doesn't want her to talk to Alec alone, so he decided to prove that she wouldn't be able to handle him if he attacked her." Joel tries to explain.

"So, he what, scared the hell out of her?" Cam pushes.

"No, he threw her back into her past." Joel bites out.

There was no need to explain it any further than that. Everyone around me knew what that single phrase meant.

It was simple, I was traumatized by what Sid had done to me, and I would probably never get over it even if I really wanted to. At least I didn't think I would get over it without the help of Marcus. I needed him here with me. He was the only one that I could be around and not be afraid.

But I was beginning to think that it was time to give up on getting Marcus back. Maybe it was time to place my heart into someone else's hands.

"Well, I know just what she needs to get back to reality." Cam grins widely.

"And what would that be?" Joel inquires with a raised brow.

"Dancing, lots and lots of dancing, how does that sound, little sister?" Cam replies as he directs his attention toward me for my response.

"Sounds like fun to me, Lass. You should come with us." Flynn chimes in as he enters the room before he steps up beside Cam.

Flynn moves closer and then places his hand against my cheek. I close my eyes and then let out a deep breath that I hadn't realized I had been holding.

My body relaxes, and I quickly feel more myself, in control, and ready to go out and have some long-overdue fun with my brother.

I nod while opening my eyes as Flynn moves away. "Dancing does sound like fun."

Bouncing on his toes, Cam moves in towards me, giving me a quick brotherly kiss on the forehead before rushing back out of the room.

"Wear something sexy, Sis." He yells back.

I groan as I look up at Joel. "So, it isn't all just going to be fun; it's going to be work too."

He sighs while nodding his head. "Yeah, but we can still enjoy ourselves."

"I guess so." I agree while placing my head against his chest once more.

****

A little while later, I find myself stuck in my room in nothing but my panties with clothes tossed haphazardly around my room.

I couldn't find a single thing that I wanted to wear.

Sitting down on my bed, I huff out a breath. I was starting to believe that it would be best if I stayed at home and lounged around like I usually did.

"Sis, are you ready to go?" Cam asks as he knocks on my door.

"I'm not going, Cam," I reply, defeated.

"Why not, Sis? What changed your mind?" He questions softly from the other side of the door.

I sigh roughly. "I just... I don't want to go."

Silence takes over our conversation until another set of footsteps stop in front of my door. I listen as whoever it is mutters to Cam before a set of footsteps leave.

Without warning, my door swings open before Mason walks in.

"Get out, Mason." I clip out as I stand and cover myself with my arms.

He shakes his head roughly while holding a bag out toward me. "I'm not leaving until you put this on and come with us."

"I don't want to go, Mason," I argue weakly, even as I snatch the bag from his hand.

He grins widely as I peek inside.

"Come on, Piper, come out with me." He pushes gently.

Glancing up at him, I pull out a sparkly silver halter dress from the bag. It was absolutely stunning.

"Did you buy this for me?" I ask in a barely there whisper.

Mason nods. "When I saw it, I knew it would look perfect on you."

Moving quickly, I try it on and then turn to face my mirror as I hold the back together.

He was right. The dress looked amazing on me.

Moving towards me, Mason takes the upper straps from my hands and ties them around my neck. His hands lightly brush against my skin, and I close my eyes.

It was hard to be this close to him and not remember the few moments we shared before Marcus came along.

I then shiver as his hands move to either side of my arms.

Opening my eyes again, I smile sadly at our reflection in the mirror.

We would have been good together and still could be if I could only give up Marcus.

"You look amazing, Sweetheart," Mason whispers as he smiles behind me.

I nod while leaning back against him. "Thank you, Mason."

"You can thank me by coming out with me tonight. You can save me a dance." He replies while grinning wider.

I nod while turning around to face him. "I want more than just one dance, and I want to ride in the limo."

"We can do whatever you want to do, Piper," Mason replies while taking my hand in his before leading me over to my bed.

He pushes me down to sit before grabbing the bag I had discarded on the floor.

To my surprise, he pulls out a pair of heels with silver lace that matched the dress. He motions for me to hold out my foot to him. I do without hesitation.

I then watch as he places the heel onto my foot before proceeding to wrap the lace in a crisscross pattern up to my knee, where he ties it into a neat bow.

Motioning for my other foot, he does the same before moving closer to me, his face mere millimeters away as he searches my eyes.

I wanted him to kiss me at that moment.

I wanted him to help me forget all about Marcus.

"Oh crap, sorry." Derek interrupts us from the doorway suddenly.

Our moment is ruined.

Mason glances back, sighing in frustration, before looking back to me as he stands to his feet while holding his hands towards me. "Are you ready to go?"

I nod and place my hands in his.

After pulling me to my feet, Mason leads me past Derek and into the hallway.

"I'm sorry, Brother." He apologizes to Mason.

"It's fine, Derek, don't worry about it," Mason replies as Derek follows us down the staircase and to the front door where Cam, Flynn, Selena, and Hannah are waiting patiently for us.

Letting go of Mason's hand, I rush to pull my sister into a hug. "When did you get here?"

"Joel just brought me about an hour or so ago." She answers while hugging me back.

I glance over to Joel, thankful for this. Having my sister here was wonderful. With her so close, I felt a little lighter, like the world wasn't crushing me.

Letting go of my sister, I'm pulled into another hug by Selena, who was Joel, Derek, and Mason's sister.

"I've missed you, Piper." She exclaims while holding me tightly.

"I missed you guys too," I reply with emotion clogging my words as I pull away from her embrace.

I was quickly being overwhelmed. I was overjoyed.

"Are you girls ready to dance?" Cam asks as he places his arms around mine and Selena's shoulders.

"I think I am now," I reply as a genuine smile spreads across my lips.

####

Made in the USA
Columbia, SC
09 June 2024

36358827R00233